To the greatest distraction,
Jake Alexander Spino Norris

STORIES

INTRODUCTION

I'm obsessed with conspiracy theories, cults, and self-contained narratives on history, life, and religion. They are real-world movements that create alternate worlds, and many of them go on to affect the real world. In one of my favorite Borges works, *Tlon, Uqbar, Orbis Tertius*[1], a potentially fictional, but fully realized, alternate world becomes an obsession for the academic community, and then society at large. By the end of the work, it has started to leak into the real world, slowly shifting reality to reflect it[2].

Conspiracy theories can have that effect. As of this writing (just before the 2020 election), radical right-wing group QAnon has spun a complex conspiracy theory based on the concept of the current president being some sort of hero. This idea, let out into the wild, has grown into a network of theories that it has absorbed, such as the anti-vaccine and alternative medicine movements. People on the opposite end of the political spectrum are unknowingly spouting its falsehoods and questioning voting for the Democratic candidate.

This theory isn't alone in affecting real-life behavior. The Russian state intelligence operatives, from the Okhrana of the Tsars to the GRU-FSB of Putin's tyranny, has been extremely good

---

[1] It can be found in English in both *Ficciones* and *Labyrinths*, two distinct translations made in 1961 but published a year apart.

[2] Spoilers for a story that was first published in 1940.

at planting conspiracy theories that target their enemies.[3] Off the top of my head, they are responsible for *The Protocols of the Elders of Zion*, the activities of HUAC under FDR[4], almost everything to do with the Roswell spy balloon crash and Area 51[5], more than half of the JFK assassination rumors[6], the CIA selling crack, Obama being a Muslim Kenyan[7], the aforementioned anti-vax movement, and Trump not being an incompetant petty toddler in an old man suit. All of them have widespread belief and have affected voting patterns and public dialogue, yet none of them are true.

This isn't to say that there aren't many conspiracies that weren't real. There actually was a Soviet infiltration of American society and government. Woody Guthrie and Algier Hiss were adamant Stalinists, for example. Most governments have plotted throughout all of human history to ethnically cleanse their neighbors through memetic methods, such as banning languages, religions, and even forced adoption, all under a humanitarian disguise. Countries you wouldn't expect, like Canada and New Zealand, are especially guilty of continuing those practices into the late 20th century. The British and French, despite being

---

[3] Their term, agitprop, is now used to describe any propaganda designed to cause unrest in favor of a political cause through the arts and culture.

[4] Which was started and run by a NKVD agent, Samuel Dickstein.

[5] In a strange twist, American counterintelligence, after fighting the idea for a bit, decided that having people think that their air base at Groom lake, home of top-secret planes like the SR-71 and the U-2, was home to hostile aliens was actually a good idea, and helped spread the idea.

[6] Dealt with in my story at the end of this book.

[7] Although they didn't start that, they ran with it.

ostensibly anti-slavery, economically backed the second American Confederacy throughout the Civil War[8].

The question becomes, what if these false theories actually were true. Then we have David Icke's lizard folk running around controlling things, Edmund Halley's hollow Earth[9], and the entire New Age movement being actually right about something. Would the world look like it does now, or would it be completely different?

In other words, what if "fake news", in the parlance of a man whose wealth is as mythical as bigfoot, was real?

Joseph Cadotte
Wilmington, NC, October 2020

---

[8] I can go down to the docks here in Wilmington, NC, and see where, 160 years ago, they bought slave-grown crops to ship home.

[9] Which John Quincy Adams sent an expedition to.

THE PYLON
Thomas Vaughn

Corporal John Dooley preferred to look at the world through the night-vision scope on his 7.62 sniper rifle. When he was not using the scope, he was wearing the goggles. This green-tinted reality and its thermal ghosts calmed his nerves. Because the devices were impractical during the daytime, he suffered severe headaches when the sun was out. Fortunately, their operations were conducted at night. That left him free to spend his days sleeping in the darkened room he rarely left before sundown.

"Hey Bill...do you ever wonder why we do this?" As Dooley spoke, he swept the desert floor with the rifle, looking for any signs of movement.

Corporal Bill Raines was manipulating the laser cutter with expert precision. He had already removed the cow's udders and genitals, producing the vague smell of grilled steak. The torch emitted its familiar sizzling sound when he started on the eyes. The surgical incisions were instantly cauterized, though there was little bleeding because the cow was already dead.

"Orders," replied Raines. The laconic Hoosier didn't like having his concentration broken when he was cutting, even though he had repeated this process hundreds of times.

"I know we have our orders, but don't you ever think about it?" As he spoke, Dooley detected movement about a quarter mile away. A man was navigating through the scrub carrying a flashlight. He had probably been attracted by the helicopter engine, though the lights had been doused. A nervous cow brayed to the east. Dooley centered the crosshairs on the target, studying its progress.

"I don't get paid to think. I get paid to cut. Why don't you ask the Doc?"

"I would, but he confuses me. All that stuff about souls and inter-dimensional rifts goes over my head."

"Well, the Doc's from space. You're gonna get that with those types," Raines grunted as he lifted the cow's head to gain access to the other eye. The animal had been killed by a cyanide dart. It was critical that no bullet wound be present on the carcass. The Doc had insisted on that.

"I guess so," said Dooley, clearly dissatisfied. "By the way, when is the last time you got paid anyway?" The man with the flashlight was coming closer.

"Look...no one forced you to sign up for black-ops. So, quit bitching."

"I'm not bitching. I'm just thinking. Don't you ever wonder about anything?"

"Yeah. Right now I'm wondering when you are going to shut the hell up so I can concentrate on cutting this cow's tongue out."

"All right. How long do you figure that's going to take?"

"I'll need about three more minutes."

Dooley gauged the distance between their position and the approaching target, then squeezed the trigger. The weapon barked once, the silencer absorbing most of the sound. The man with the flashlight dropped and did not move. It was a clean headshot.

"What was that?" asked Raines, not even bothering to look up from his cutting.

"Just some dumbass rancher."

Somewhere in the distance a dog barked. Dooley let the crosshairs linger over the target, then continued probing the terrain for new threats. While he hummed to himself, Raines sealed the organs in plastic containers and put them in his pack. The two men low walked back to the waiting helicopter. The darkened machine blended seamlessly with the moonless night. As the soldiers stepped on board, Raines gave the thumbs-up to the pilot and they lifted gracefully into the air like a barn owl. It paused once over the scrubland, allowing the occupants to collect the dead farmer. The cow's carcass watched them retreat to the west through sightless sockets.

After helping Raines stow the organs, Dooley donned his familiar night vision goggles and the two men settled in for the ride back to the Pylon. At first neither man spoke. Raines stared out of the window irritably, trying to ignore his colleague who regarded him through the infra-red scope projecting from his head. For several minutes, nothing could be heard but the steady strum of the prop blade.

"I know you don't want to talk about it, but here's another question. Why do we have to do it this way? Why can't we just keep the cows at the Pylon? You know...like raise our own. Why do we have to come all the way out here? This is such a pain in the ass. We're not getting any younger and I've got a bum knee."

"Christ, Dooley! How the hell should I know? Maybe there isn't enough room at the Pylon to raise cattle."

Dooley shrugged. It was a puzzle. But then again, much about his life was puzzling. He watched the desert unfold beneath him under the ghostly enhancement of the infrared. He longed for the darkness of his room at the Pylon. Raines kept his legs braced against the cow organs underneath his seat, careful to keep the contents from shifting.

After about thirty minutes, the Pylon's beacon came into view. The building had received its name because of its bizarre shape. It was a series of interconnected outbuildings surrounding a large, tapering cone that jutted over one hundred feet in the air. Despite its size, the canyon walls that rose on three sides obscured it from view. It was two hundred miles to the nearest interstate.

When they touched down, the two occupants disembarked with their cargo and walked toward a large steel door. Raines clutched the organs against his chest as if they were his children. Neither man spoke to the pilot as they had long ago forgotten his name.

The Doc was waiting for them at the entrance. His face turned bright red with anticipation and the air bladder at his throat expelled gas with flatulent resonance. The lab coat was ill-fitted for his short, wide frame. The redness of his scales intensified. His color always changed when he became agitated.

"Was the cow pregnant?" he asked, twisting his tentacles around one another with nervous anticipation.

"I don't think so," replied Raines, handing over the plastic container.

"Didn't you read my memo?" The air bladder made another farting noise.

Raines and Dooley looked at one another, then shook their heads.

"How in the hell are we going to complete the transfer of consciousness without the appropriate generative tissues? The anima mundi exists at all points of space and time as a singularity. I am convinced the cellular matrix of the developing fetus contains the code. Do you know how close we are to having an organic receptor capable of interpreting the rift? I left a note for you in the breakroom."

Dooley wagged his finger in the air. "Yeah. I did see something. Do you mean that crayon drawing of the headless frog sitting at the center of a wheel with light radiating in all directions? The one that said THE ANSWER IS IN THE MEAT at the top?"

"Yes, damnit!"

"Well, I didn't know what that meant."

The Doc stepped toward Dooley, staring into the lens that jutted in front of the soldier's face. As his body undulated beneath the bloodstained research garment his narrow eyes seemed to swell in Dooley's infrared field. The bladder exhaled once again.

"We need to work on our communication. This project won't go anywhere until the two of you evolve enough to decode metaphorical language. We are light years beyond the linguistic boys. You best get with the program."

With that the Doc stomped off with the organs, his tail leaving a noticeable blood smear on the stained linoleum. The two men didn't say anything for a while. Finally Dooley turned to Raines and smiled.

"Well, I guess that rancher isn't going to bury himself."

It was days like this that Major Jim Sparks regretted his appointment as a business operations auditor. His teeth rattled as the SUV bounced along a supply road that wasn't much more than a game trail. The sun beat against the glass like an enraged animal. Last week it had been the sweltering heat of Savannah, Georgia, where the army was running coke through Mexico. Today it was the barren womb of New Mexico.

"This must be some top secret stuff to be way out here, if you don't mind me saying so, Sir." The lieutenant was named Jenks. He seemed like a nice enough kid. There was no doubt he had the right connections since he had gotten the highest security clearance fresh out of West Point. He had probably selected operations auditing for the same reason everyone else did. Once you learned how the money flowed through the back channels of the Pentagon, it made you a highly sought after commodity in the defense industry after you retired.

"Maybe. The truth is I have no idea. They call it the Pylon."

"Why do they call it that, Sir?"

"You'll know when you see it. The Air Force originally owned the land. They wanted to use it for that nuclear powered jet back in the fifties. When that project went ass up, we inherited it."

"Jeez," said the lieutenant as a large stone rebounded abruptly off the chassis. "Sorry, Sir. I don't see how supply vehicles make it up this road."

"They get deliveries once every two months. It's just enough traffic to keep the brush clear."

"And you don't know what they're doing, Major?"

"Lieutenant...do you have any idea how much shit flies under the radar with a trillion dollar budget? These black-ops are like gopher warrens when it comes to funding. Sometimes a place can switch operation templates so many times even we lose track of what we're paying for."

"Are there any records?"

"Not too many. The most recent one I found was a mimeographed report, which should tell you how outdated it was. It was an offshoot of MKUltra back when we were still horsing around with new interrogation techniques. They took a few of those Berkeley radicals the FBI had been rounding up for bombing post offices and sequestered them in the desert. The R&D boys had created a new derivative of LSD called CI249. It was part of a classification of drugs called Cerebral Inhibitors. They were supposed to short-circuit psychic defenses, leaving the brain more susceptible to suggestion. The idea was to reform those longhairs into good little boys and girls who would recite the Pledge of Allegiance at the drop of a hat."

"I heard about that sort of thing. Why didn't they just waterboard them?"

"Because everything has to be complicated, Lieutenant. The more complicated an operation is, the more expensive. If your project isn't absorbing enough money, those asshats in Washington start to think you're not doing anything."

As the SUV rounded a sandstone ridge, the road leveled out. Nestled between the canyon walls sat the Pylon. It looked like someone had stacked a lighthouse on top of a strip mall. The bleached concrete shimmered under waves of heat distortion. The perimeter was protected by nothing but razor wire and desolation.

"I see what you mean about the name, Sir," said the lieutenant. "It looks like an outdated reactor design. Are you sure it's manned?"

"Well, someone has been signing for the shipments of food, clothes, and fuel. To be honest, I expect this is nothing more than a warehouse for chemical weapons or something."

As the SUV approached the Pylon, both men fell silent. There was no way they could know that they were driving over the bones of forgotten Apaches who once scraped a living from the unforgiving desert and the dead Mexicans that had ventured up from Sonora to mine mercury. The desert had a way of swallowing people. Once it digested you, there was nothing left. The memories of entire civilizations had been completely obliterated.

About a quarter mile from the entrance, they saw a vulture standing astride the carcass of a dead longhorn. There was nothing left but hide and bleached bones. The skin was stretched across the ribs like an obscene tent. As they passed, the vulture bobbed its head as if in greeting.

When the SUV paused at the entrance, a man wearing fatigues and sunglasses stared at them for several seconds before opening the gate. He appeared confused. Perspiration was beaded on his face. As he came alongside the vehicle, the lieutenant rolled the window down.

"We're not expecting supplies this week."

"We're not the chow wagon, soldier," said the major. "We're in from Washington. We have orders to audit your operations."

The man studied the two occupants of the vehicle as if they were some type of cypher. "Operations? Right...Operations." There was a long pause before he added, "Sir." It was as if the word had to be dredged from some long disused tomb. He signaled them through. The two men in the SUV were unaware when their vehicle bumped over the top of the rancher's shallow grave as they passed through the gate.

"Major? Did you see that man's uniform? Isn't he a little old to be a private?"

"I noticed that. He can't be a day younger than fifty." He glanced at the landing pad. "At least they're keeping the bird in good shape. You don't see many Blackhawks these days. It seems to be outfitted for night surveillance. You know what that means."

"No, Sir. I don't."

"That means things just got complicated."

As the two men exited the SUV, the heat pounded against their shoulders like a vengeful child. The blast of hot wind was a shock after the air-conditioned vehicle. A crude Eye of Sirius was painted over the door to the barracks.

"What in the hell?" muttered Sparks under his breath. "Private, where is your commanding officer?"

The guard looked confused and rubbed his chin nervously. A fly alit on his forehead, but he didn't seem to notice. "I don't know. It could be Dooley. Maybe it's Raines. We all take orders from the Doc."

Sparks consulted his file. "Are you talking about Corporal Robert Dooley and Corporal William Raines?"

"I'm not sure. I just know them as Dooley and Raines. I didn't know they had first names, but I guess it makes sense they would."

"Major," whispered Lieutenant Jenks. "This man doesn't seem right to me. It's like he's not all there."

"Yeah. No shit," replied Sparks, then turned back to the private. "Maybe you better introduce us to Dooley and Raines."

The guard seemed relieved. He clearly felt burdened by human interaction.

"Why is this eye painted over the door, soldier?" inquired Jenks as they entered the building.

"That's to remind us that the Doc is always watching."

"And who is the Doc?"

"He's the one who runs this place."

"On whose authority?"

The man cast a confused glance at the lieutenant. "Well, the Doc's from space."

The two officers were led to a breakroom where they seated themselves to wait for Dooley and Raines. The hallways were narrow and dimly lit. It was immediately apparent there was no air-conditioning and the paint seemed to be melting from the walls. Asbestos tiles hung from the ceiling. It almost looked abandoned.

"Sir," said Jenks. "Do you see that calendar on the wall? It's from 1992."

"Something deeply perverse has happened here, son. I want you to keep your eyes peeled."

"Yes Sir. Do you know these two boys we're about to interrogate?"

"No, but their names are on the original registry."

"What?"

"That's right. I knew the bureaucracy was dense, but this is a black hole of epic proportions. I don't think these men have left this base in over twenty-five years. I've got a Colonel Caldwell listed as the head of operations for the CI249 trials. I wonder what the hell happened to him. By the way, do you have your sidearm?"

As the question slipped from Sparks' mouth, his ears popped with a loud explosion. Beside him, the lieutenant's head jerked backwards and cranial matter splattered the wall. The major felt a wash of warm fluid on his shoulder, his body tensing imperceptibly. He glanced to the doorway and saw a soldier holding a rifle, his lips peeled back in a sneer. Everything slowed. He had never been in combat and wondered if this was what it was like. One minute you are talking to someone and the next their brains are painted on the side of your face. As the cortisol began to course through his system, he maintained just enough detachment to study the situation. He noticed the man's name tag. The only way to stay alive was to assert his authority.

"Corporal Raines!" he barked. "Are you aware you just murdered a superior officer of the United States Army?!"

"The man he shot was an intruder who entered these premises without authorization."

It was not the soldier who spoke, but a bloated man with long gray hair tied in a ponytail standing behind him. His lab coat was covered in blood. There was a large, tumorous goiter on one side of his neck that seemed to pulse beneath an unidentifiable skin disease. He squinted at the major through porcine eyes, his breath coming in short rattles.

"Are you Caldwell?" asked Sparks, watching the barrel of the rifle, wondering if he had any chance of reaching his dead colleague's pistol.

"Caldwell?" mused the man in the lab coat. "I haven't heard that name in a while, but I remember him. He definitely wasn't with it."

The major studied the strange, deformed man in the doorway. There was a nagging familiarity in his misshapen features. Then the image from the dossier flashed through his mind.

"You're John Croften," said the major with sudden realization. "You were with the Underground New World Order. You bombed that armory in Baltimore. They gave you twenty years."

"Should I plug him, Doc?" asked Raines and the weapon centered between Sparks' eyes. The major felt his sphincter tighten.

"No. Not yet," said the man in the lab coat, stepping around the corporal. "To answer your question, I was John Croften. But he's been gone for a long time. Things have changed now that I can see."

Sparks turned toward Raines, trying to make eye contact with him. He noticed that the man's pupils were vibrating back and forth. "Corporal...it is my belief that this man is supposed to be your prisoner. Try to remember. You were engaged in a drug experiment designed to treat people with un-American values. It appears you have been contaminated by the Cerebral Inhibitor. You are suffering from a psychotic delusion."

"The Doc's from space," said the soldier through gritted teeth.

"No, he isn't. He is an unrepentant, degenerate communist."

The major watched as the man's finger tightened on the trigger and he figured the hand had been overplayed. Whatever this man was before he had been introduced to CI249, it was gone now. But the Doc placed a restraining hand on his shoulder.

"Not yet. Let's show the major what we've been up to. It's the least we can do. After all, he's the one paying for all of this."

Raines motioned with the barrel of the rifle and Sparks rose, his hands in the air. He was guided into a dingy hallway where another armed soldier waited, his eyes blinking spasmodically.

"What's his problem?" asked Sparks.

"Oh...that's Dooley. He doesn't like coming out in the daytime. The light bothers his eyes."

As they moved further down the corridor, a wretched stench assaulted the major's senses. It smelled like a mixture of decaying flesh, vomit, and bleach.

"It's all about getting rid of your ego," the Doc was saying. "That's the only way you can truly see. You've got to leave all that baggage behind. I've plugged into the anima mundi. The universe is just one big soul. Space is just one big chain of molecular consciousness. John Croften is dead. You know why?" He cast a yellowed grin over his shoulder and pointed to his forehead. "It's all in here. The universal soul has been downloaded into me. I'm space, man...you dig?"

"You're insane," interjected Sparks, but his voice carried less conviction. He tried desperately to maintain the veneer of authority. Perhaps one of these men still possessed some vestige of who they had been. Maybe he could resurrect that dead self like a dormant revenant. But as he walked by the rooms that lined the corridor, his confidence slipped. Trash was piled in the corners and lightbulbs flickered overhead. It was close to a hundred degrees and his uniform clung to his skin. Roach carcasses crunched underfoot. He never imagined that soldiers of the United States Army would allow themselves to live in such degraded conditions. The two men that flanked him on either side reminded him of guards leading a condemned man to the gallows.

"They're going to come looking for me, you lunatic."

"Right," said the Doc, his voice laced with sarcasm. "This is a black hole. You dig? We don't exist. That means you don't exist as long as you're here. You think a phalanx of gunships are going to come flying to your rescue just because you're wearing a few bars? Get real. You'll disappear. You'll end up in a plane crash on your way to Guam or some type of BS like that. You're in the belly of the beast."

The words stung Sparks because he knew they were true. When the money trail vanished, so did you. Bile in his stomach began to rise as the stench became unbearable.

"My God...how can you stand that smell?"

"It's the smell of freedom, brother," said the Doc, pushing open the doors at the end of the hallway. "You know it's sad that you call this place the Pylon. A pylon is a stationary obstruction. That's not what it is now. It's the total opposite. This is the tip of the spear. We've got places to go."

There was nothing that could have prepared Sparks for what he saw. A mass of heaving flesh sat at the center of the circular chamber. Tubes hung from its flanks, pumping preservatives into the decaying flesh. At various points, active electrodes had been inserted and the mass of organic material spasmed as if in pain. It was ringed by a circle of dark, bovine eyes. As the thing twitched Sparks saw a number of attendants moving about the room as if they were acolytes attending some obscene goddess. They injected fluids and applied electricity to rotting muscle tissue.

Whether or not they were former soldiers or prisoners was impossible to tell. The major felt his knees go weak.

"What is that?" he asked in a rasping voice.

"Can't you tell? We're getting out of here. I've got the galactic consciousness downloaded into my brain, but I can't get us off this rock. The human mind doesn't have the juice. This will be my vehicle for projecting matter into space. See the uteruses at the center? They represent the womb of the universe. We sewed eyes around the edge because you have to be able to see where you're going."

As the man in the tainted lab coat ranted, he pointed out various details of the sickening project. "And the tongues? Do we not speak our universe into being moment to moment? That's how God did it in the Bible. We're going to use the mother womb to speak a new reality. Then we can go wherever we want. We're going to fly like eagles."

"But..." whispered the major. "These are just pilfered cow organs."

The Doc stared at the major for a moment. "You would say something like that." There was a profound disappointment in his voice. "Hey Dooley. Hit the lights."

One of the men flipped the light panel and the room went dark. As he did so, the major became aware of the long cone extending above his head. They were in the Pylon itself. What appeared to be various star clusters had been painted on the side of the wall in radium, extending all the way to the ceiling. The constellations glowed under the black light. He began to experience a sickening sense of vertigo as he stared upward. The Doc retrieved a laser pointer.

"This is our navigational chart. Once we activate the cellular awareness of the world soul, I will use my galactic consciousness to project us through space. Alpha Centauri. The Belt of Orion. The Crab Nebulae."

As the man narrated the glyphs on the wall, Major Sparks looked back at the tortured mass of flesh on the table. He focused on a singular tongue twitching obscenely in the air. His vision began to darken and he slumped to his knees.

"Vega. Rigel. This here is Pluto, but I'm not sure we can get the planets to line up right once we take off. We might have to skip those."

That's when the major retched the contents of his stomach onto the floor. When his stomach was empty, he looked around at the luminescent destinations that lined the crude star chamber, a strip of drool hanging from the side of his lip. He tried to wrap his mind around the delusional psychosis that had gripped this station. A profound desire to flee the Pylon galvanized in his muscles. He looked toward the exit. The man they called Dooley was staring into his face through night vision headgear. All of the agitation that Sparks had noted earlier was gone. The man looked utterly calm—almost serene. Then the major noticed the barrel of the pistol Dooley was now pointing at him, right between his eyes.

"Polaris, man. We can't miss out on Polaris. It's all about projecting your awareness," droned the Doc, no longer paying any attention to the major. The madman was lost in his own cosmic exposition.

A dreamy smile drifted across Dooley's lips.

"Sorry you can't make the trip, Major," he whispered in a kind voice.

Sparks did not realize it when his own awareness was blown from his body. Drops of his blood splattered the wall, creating a new constellation for the travelers to ponder when they were ready to make that final leap across the beckoning void.

BACKGROUND FOR
THE PYLON

Where did the cattle mutilation conspiracy originate and what are some useful sources?

Rumors of strange cattle mutilations persisted in the American Southwest and Midwest through the 1970s. In 1980, environmental journalist Linda Moulton Howe produced a documentary called *Strange Harvest* that took the cattle mutilation theory to the national stage. The theory that extraterrestrial beings or government agencies were using sophisticated techniques to amputate portions of privately owned cattle became fairly mainstream at this point. This belief was further augmented by *Endangered Species* (1982), starring Robert Urich and Jobeth Williams in a movie that was a likely inspirational candidate for the *X-Files*. These theories persist despite the efforts of researchers who have demonstrated that scavengers and natural decay processes often produce cleanly cut, bloodless wounds.

What did you change and what is the fallout?

I didn't really change the theory, other than to provide an explanatory framework. I tried to stay true to both the government and extraterrestrial angles. This theory emerged at the end of the Cold War. The United States government was increasingly being seen as a source of threat to its own citizens, rather than as a benevolent protector. It has contributed to the ongoing belief that all-powerful, malevolent forces are at work that threaten people's safety. Theories like this one continue to reverberate in a cultural psyche that is now increasingly reliant on delusional thinking.

What attracted you to this period/theory?
This theory was widespread when I was a kid. While I was still young and impressionable, the idea just didn't make sense. I could not figure out why the government would mutilate privately owned cattle. Why not simply create their own farm? The same question comes into play with advanced extraterrestrials. It was one of the first times I can remember using my critical thinking skills to challenge a belief that the majority of those around me took for granted. The challenge of a story like The Pylon is how to come up with an explanation as to why anyone would use such an expensive and inefficient method to experiment on cattle.

What is a good introduction to the period?
Wall of Voodoo's *Call of the West*.

THE LAST INVADER

Elizabeth Kidder

The car won't start. Again. Even inside the car, I can see my breath. A long, aggressive sigh escapes me and I hope, against odds, that it's the battery, an easy fix.

It's never the battery.

I refuse to open the hood, knowing that the minute the internal mechanisms become visible, my day will become twice as hard, and walk back inside to get my leathers. Evan is still asleep, and the annoyed part of me wants to make a noise, stomp in the boots and jingle the keys so someone else shares my impotent frustration. But I just write a note on the whiteboard that hasn't been white since we got it, and slip back outside. Moments later, I'm flying down the road on the motorcycle, all the layers in the world worthless against the stinging threads of winter air finding every crack in my helmet's mask.

It's a forty-minute drive, lonely in the dawn, the roar of the bike drowning out everything but my internal worrying. The litany starts up again: find non-existent time to wash the dishes in the sink so we can use forks again instead of spoons, find non-existent emotional bandwidth to help my patients, and now find non-existent money in the budget to fix the car. Billboards start to fly by as I get closer to town, selling me things I need and can't afford, along with the obligatory "GET YOURSELF TREATED" government signage in bold red letters on reflective white circles. While I hate being unable to listen to music on the bike, I'm a little grateful for the lack of talk-news radio pundits waxing on about the potential outcomes of the invasion, over ten years after it ended. Fear mongers. Like any of them have visited a treatment center to see the true aftermath first hand.

I pull into the parking lot, nearly empty this early, and snag the first spot—a small victory. I try to build onto that when I walk in and find a chocolate cake doughnut left over in the nearly empty box we got yesterday, and—third time's the charm—only two new patient folders waiting in my inbox. I find a place to rest my helmet on top of the filing cabinets, and hold the doughnut in my mouth as I strip off my boots and change into more appropriate attire. I suppose my clients wouldn't care what I wear, but my coworkers would. That's why I come in so early—not only do I get to leave early, but I also get to avoid the drama of office gossip.

Finally able to enjoy my doughnut, I finish entering paperwork I left from yesterday, and flip through the new files. Transfers from another city—only new to me, just looking to treat their existing symptoms. Despite what the talking heads and tabloids want you to believe, there have been no new cases since the invasion. I grab today's schedule and head to the observation room. Despite the soothing blue walls, elegant light sconces, and white leather sofa and armchairs, the room is nothing but clinical to me. I've been here for six years—I know the smell of ammonium cleaner and lemon masking vomit and blood when I encounter it.

I sign into the computer and pull up my first patient—Greg Tandry. Greg has been seeing me every other week for the past three years. He always feels close to a breakthrough, and I wonder why he hasn't shaken it yet. Otherwise pleasant and friendly, it's an easy way to start the day. Another button, and the twin scanners descend from the ceiling, coming to a stop above central armchair. I wipe the handles down, as well as the headrest and arms of the chair, always more careful around the fingernail scratches in the leather—we aren't getting new funding any time soon. I hear a tap from the wall of glass behind me, and turn to see the two-way mirror turned off, revealing the observation deck—chairs, equipment control panels, and Lisa, the government agent assigned to our clinic. She waves, and points to the clock behind her, then the window returns to a mirror. Almost eight—time to start the day.

Greg is right on time. While we get the equipment honed to his frequency, we chat about inane topics—weather, traffic, anything with less substance than a chocolate doughnut. It's important that the patient is as relaxed and open as possible before starting a session, and knowing what's in store for him, I don't want to dive into anything heavy before I'm in a position to medically help him.

"Alright, Greg. Notice any unusual behaviors recently?"

He pauses a second, running through his week, but I'm not surprised that he eventually shakes his head.

"Just my wife's," he jokes weakly. I smile at the familiar jab. Even before their trial separation over a month ago, I think he saw me more often than he saw Camille. Once the routine questions are out of the way, I sit down across from him and pull out the control tablet from the arm of the chair, a simplified version of the various machines in the room behind me, where Lisa is now sitting. It shows brain waves, heart rate, and other knowledge collected from the scanners encircling his head. Right now, everything reads normal. That's unlikely to change. Greg is as placid as a winter lake.

"Greg, I'd like to go back to last week's session. We talked about what happened at the park. I'd like to explore that more. Could you tell me if this episode felt different from others you've had in the past?"

"You mean, stronger, or longer?"

"Anything at all that seems to make it stand out in your mind."

"No, it felt pretty similar. The words were different, but they always are. It felt like normal, like I wasn't in control anymore." He laughs a little. "Imagine, losing control being normal. It didn't used to be this way." His smile fades, never really having a chance against the sadness under his skin.

I smile sympathetically. "I think you're really close to a breakthrough, Greg. You've been diligent about your visits, and your episodes are fewer and farther between, with less severity each time."

"None of that seems to matter much, when it happens," he says. "All these years working with you, all for nothing when it takes over. And with Camille moving back in with her mother, it makes me feel like...giving in."

I weigh my next words carefully. "Ultimately, that's your decision," I say. "I can't make you do anything you don't want to do. But I hope you know, the same applies to you. You have all the power within you to conquer this on your own." I lean back in the chair. "You're just here so I have someone to talk to besides myself." This time, his smile is genuine.

The rest of the session proceeds as normal. After evaluation, we go through our concentration and centering exercises, and I write him a prescription for his weekly supplement. I wish I could do them once a month with my regulars—less paperwork and phone calls for me—but Lisa would have my ass for giving clients that much unfettered access to such powerful psychotropic drugs. There's a reason we can only legally prescribe one pill a week. When I tested a half dose back in med school, my brain felt like violin strings being plucked—everything taut and vibrating with energetic sound. It took half a week before I felt back to normal.

Greg's tidy sessions mean quick post-visit reviews with Lisa. We compare vitals to last week's session, and add a few notes to Greg's electronic file. The park incident had worried me—after weeks of calm, so much that I considered marking him in remission, he'd suddenly stripped down to his underwear and went streaking through the playground. Luckily, no kids had been around at that late hour, but more than a few adults had, and it took testimonies from both Lisa and myself that he was not a risk factor in a public setting, and should continue his sessions in lieu of time served. Greg was lucky. Not all of the affected had a good track record.

Liam Stadtler was one of the new patients coming in today. Over a package of chips from the vending machine, I read through his file. Since diagnosis in his teens nearly a decade ago, he'd jumped from treatment center to treatment center, with month long gaps in his records before he'd pop up in a new city. The notes do not look promising—sullen, taciturn, and anger issues. I smiled in spite of myself. A challenge.

"Liam, nice to meet you. I'm Doctor Adrian Shale." He doesn't accept my hand or my offering, instead choosing to stare at the two-way mirror.

"I'm looking forward to working with you in your journey towards recovery. From your records, I see you are quite familiar with the procedures, so let's just get started. Have you exhibited any unusual behaviors recently?"

He doesn't offer any, but his file talks about outbursts in public, loud arguments with himself and those around him.

"Have you experienced any desires that are not your own?"

That gets a reaction—an unsettling grin, quickly removed and replaced by an uncomfortable frown.

"Any voices that do not seem to belong to you?"

"Of course there are," he finally speaks. "Ten years of it. Guess I've gotten used to it."

"It's all right to have these slip ups," I reassure him. "It's part of the healing process. But I don't want you to let these incidents become routine. It's a serious problem that needs to be addressed."

A slight spike in the vitals. I've hit a nerve, as I'd hoped. "I know it's serious. That's why I'm here."

"Yes, you are," I nod, purposefully maintaining eye contact. "And yet, these episodes have persisted for years. Don't you want to be rid of them?"

"I don't really have a say in that matter, now do I?" His voice is hollow and hopeless, and yet his eyes shine.

"What if you did have a say in it? What would you do?"

"Too long, too long. What would I do without it now? No matter how loud I scream, I can't drown it out, but it's the only thing that's been there for me, all these years."

"You can't depend on something that isn't there."

His jaw tightens and his eyes roll back into his head. The spikes erupt in a flurry of warning beeps. I hear two taps on the glass behind me—Lisa. I don't go for the anesthesia though. First impressions are everything.

"I. Am. Here," intones Liam, but guttural, lower than his speaking voice. A common expression of the psychosis. His eyes have refocused on me, pupils dilated, carotid artery pulsating wildly.

"I know you're here, Liam," I say calmly.

"I know this!" he shouts. "I've been here, molding him, shaping him. Even as he resists me, I continue to try and help him. But Liam is weak." He leans forward towards me. "Not like you."

"Liam, I need you to try and clear your mind. You are experiencing a break. There is no one else here, besides us two."

"You know that isn't true," Liam spits, saliva flowing down his chin. "As much as I know there is a person behind that mirror. I can see how long you've observed my kind. You are aware that we are more than these suits of flesh."

"Liam," I insist. "You are ill. That is all this is—a manifestation of your disease."

"I am not a disease!" And he lunges at me.

It's been a while since I've had a fighter, and I'm a little stiff with the syringe hidden within the pen with which I've been taking notes, a standard issue for therapists in my field. Loading it each day had become as rote as washing my hands, and it had been years since I've had to use it in session. I'm pleased to see that last year's re-certification is fresh enough that I manage not to stab myself as I adjust the pen in my hand and side step his lunge to inject his arm with anesthesia. Still fueled by anger, he spins and reaches for me, but his momentum is my advantage. I lay my hands on his shoulders and continue to spin him, then wrap my arms around his and link my hands behind his shoulder blades. "Liam, I am here!" I say with a calm strength. "Relax. I am here." He continues to flail as I bring him down to the ground, but Lisa is in the room at that point, and wraps her arms around his thighs to further restrain him.

His movements grow weaker, more sluggish. "I am here," I say again, and I hear him say, "Stop...you're...hurting us..." before he goes slack into unconsciousness. The alarms continue to wail in the background, and Lisa and I lock eyes, still wary of releasing our hold on the prone body.

They call it brain rot on the news, but the technical term is viral psychosis. It can't be treated with antibiotics like other diseases, and while it doesn't appear to have a lasting effect on the body beyond feverish symptoms from the initial infection, it manifests in psychotic breaks from reality, ranging from benign to dangerous. The most common indicators are expressions of dissociative identity disorder, with the subject appearing to exhibit other personalities. Through therapy and medication, the effects can be subdued, and eventually the psychosis can be considered in remission, but the longer the symptoms persist, the harder it is to cure. Liam's case is one of the oldest I've seen, and the gaps in treatment are dangerous for a long-term case like his. The less treatment he receives, the less likely he'll ever be free of it.

We place Liam in one of the recovery rooms and go back to the observation deck. Lisa gets me a glass of water, and I quickly drink it down.

"You should have sedated him sooner," she admonishes me.

"I needed to see what level we were dealing with," I say between long sips.

"You were too close to losing control," she says. "It's been a long time since you've treated a fighter."

"I've received the same training as you," I reply.

"I know you have," she says, and I'm worried to hear a note of concern in her voice. Lisa is always stoic, always practical. She only shows emotion when she's anxious.

"Good news is, we know what we're dealing with," I say quickly. "We'll be able to be more cautious during our next session."

"If he comes back."

She has a point, but I'm quick to deflect. "He does seem to be a flight risk. Let's keep him in Room C over the weekend, just to run some more diagnostics. I want to form our own opinions on his condition."

"Agreed." Her stoicism has returned, and I inwardly sigh in relief. Lisa has been a constant since I came here three years ago. I don't want that to change. We compare our notes from Liam's session, and write up a detailed report for the weekend therapist, as well as itinerary and medicinal schedule for the night nurses. After that large an episode, Liam will be kept sedated for the majority of the weekend, and I move next week's schedule around to make sure I see him on Monday.

Then it's back to the rest of the day's clients. The hours pass by quickly after so much excitement, and before I know it, I'm waving goodbye to Lisa and heading out to the bike. The evening is a little warmer, but the sun is getting low in the sky already, and I quickly speed down the road.

A slightly cool dinner is waiting on the stovetop for me when I get home, along with a note.

Got a ride with Marcus, see you later, Evan
P.S. I love your face.

Despite the broken car and the long day, I can't help but crack a smile. I grab the empanadas he made and a glass of ice water, and go sit down in the den, the last rays of sunlight streaming through the high windows. The evening light through the stained glass makes this room my favorite, and I take in our shelves of records, the piles of throw blankets and floor pillows, the murals we've painted on the wall—our home, our life. The only thing missing is Evan, but he's rarely home at this time of day. I'm still feeling flushed from the ride, so I crack open a panel of the window and lay down beside it on the settee, feeling the icy breeze play across my face. I contemplate going upstairs to bed to get an early night's sleep so I can be awake when Evan gets home, but in the end, I'm too tired to even close the window as I drift off to sleep.

I awake to Evan's voice and see him closing the window. "Addy, what were you thinking?" he admonishes me. "It's freezing outside!"

But I don't feel cold. I feel warm, and I would open the window again if I wasn't so tired. "What time is it?"

"It's almost two in the morning. I thought you'd be in bed by now."

"Well, I was sleeping," I say contrarily, and am rewarded with an exasperated smile. I take it, and try to drag myself to my feet. "Too tired...to move..."

This time, a sigh, and he pulls a blanket over me. He knows better than to try and carry me to bed—I tend to hit a lot of doorframes with my extremities. I hear him sit down in the armchair next to me, and then darkness again.

Hungry.
I wake up, famished. I don't even stop to see what time it is before I open the fridge and pull out a grapefruit and frozen toaster strudel. I put the strudel in the toaster and tear open the grapefruit impatiently, eating over half of it before the strudel pops out, golden and hot. I grab it with my other hand, not minding the burns on my fingertips and tongue as I devour it.

The food is gone in less than a minute, and I gulp down half of the milk carton.

Clean.

I look down at the smears of jelly and juice drips on the counter, the crumbs on the floor, the dirty dishes in the sink, and can't stand another minute of the unclean kitchen. I pull out white rags, dish soap, and an apron. Evan staggers into the kitchen to find me mid-scrub on the floor, the front of my apron soaked in soap from cleaning dishes, and half the tile floor ruthlessly polished.

"Addy?"

"Yeah?" I say, still pulling the rag back and forth across the floor.

Cabinets.

I turn to see grease stains and coffee grounds on the wooden doors, something I hadn't yet noticed. Guess those are my next project.

"What are you doing?"

"Cleaning the floor. Cabinets next."

"Yeah, I can see that. Let me rephrase—why are you doing this at five in the morning?"

"You're right, that is a better way to ask it. Step back, please," I ask as the rag grazes the tips of his toes.

"So...why?"

"It was on my list. If I'm fast enough, I can get to the car before sunrise."

"You sure you don't want to come back to bed? With me?"

Want.

I stop dead in my tracks, and look up at his stubbled jawline, mussed hair, wrinkled black shirt, and nearly leap up from the floor. It's unfair for him to look that good on three hours of sleep.

"Definitely," I say seriously. "But let me finish up here. You go back to bed, I'll be back soon."

He gives me a funny look, but turns to go back to bed. "Wait!" I call after him, and when he turns back, I throw him a spare towel. "For dusting the ceiling fan."

That gets a sigh.

The cold doesn't even bother me as I unclip the jumper cables. Miracle of miracles, it was just the battery. I wipe a little bit of fluid off my hands, but don't put the gloves back on. Even the winter air feels pleasant. I hope I'm not growing sentimental. I look up at the second floor window and wonder if Evan is still awake.

Let us find out.

I take the stairs two a time, but pause before I put my hand on the bedroom door. He needs his sleep. And I can get more done around the house. What if he isn't in the mood still?

Do not worry.

Not worry? Who do I think I am? That's not like me.

Wait...

That's not like me.

That's NOT me.

Correct.

I blink, and the world around me splits, chasms opening in the walls and spiderwebbing across the door. I stifle a scream and feel my legs fold up under me.

Stop.

No.

I can't keep the whimper inside on that one. It's not possible

It happened.

"Stop," I whisper this time, tight and strangled.

Why?

I hear movement behind the door. I have to leave.

Stay.

And a part of me wants to stay, to tell Evan that the unthinkable has happened, that I'm no longer myself, that nothing will ever be the same, and let his wonderful optimism bubble me up and keep me afloat with kind words and unshakeable faith. And then reality pierces my brain, and I flee down the stairs, into a coat and jacket, and out into the icy dawn.

Cold. Frost. Rabbit. Grass. Wind.

I try to ignore the litany as the landscape whips by, but who ever escaped from the voices inside their head? I shouldn't even be operating a motor vehicle while experiencing an episode, but I have no other choice to get back to clinic for treatment.

Not sick.

I now admire Greg's self control. If this kept going for too much longer, I would've done a lot more than strip in a park.

Not. Sick.

More emphatic this time. I would've hoped my consciousness would be a bit more rational under these conditions, knowing as much as I do about the symptoms.

STOP.

The word is as solid as a brick wall, and the motorcycle skids to a halt on the empty road. I manage to unclench my fists and stare at them like they aren't my own. I did not tell them to brake, and that makes me nervous. Loss of control over motor functions is a very severe reaction.

Need to talk.

I pull the bike off the road, and sit down on a fallen fence beam, ignoring the frost. Concentration and will are necessary for recovery. I've helped hundreds of patients, I can help myself.

I force my inner thoughts to be silent, clench and unclench my fingers, my toes, my teeth, straining for silence.

Talk.

I will not.

Then listen.

I hum quietly to myself.

Bastard.

Bastard? I haven't used that epithet since grade school.

Pick another.

I'd rather not. Why am I engaging with my own delusion?

Not delusion. From beyond. From above. Sent here.

There is a lot of talk about what the aliens wanted with us when they arrived at Earth ten years ago. We had hoped the first species to find us in the galaxy would be peaceful. They had seemed to be so, though we never saw them physically. All we ever saw was the strange transmission device they sent down to us from their bright ship hovering above in the stratosphere. Despite several attempts, we never could translate much beyond a greeting. Then the first cases of viral psychosis appeared. Further attempts to communicate with the aliens were futile, and just as suddenly as they had arrived, their ship of lights returned to the stars. They never returned, and we never got any answers. We couldn't even tell if it was an act of biological warfare, or if, like natives meeting with settlers from across the sea, they had even been aware they had brought it with them.

We knew what we did.

That was a complete sentence. A shiver racks my body.

Cold.

I'm fine.

Afraid.

I'm. Fine.

You will be.

I want that to be true. I need it to be true. I take another deep breath, and stare at my hands, and the black cracks streaming from between my clenched fingers.

Everything will be fine.

I've never been happier for the helmet's mask as I scream.

The clinic isn't open yet, and there is an eerie quiet in the still air of the hallway. Even the patients aren't awake. I can hear the quiet beeping of the monitors as I walk to my office.

Why are we here?

I'll have to wait till I see Lisa on Monday to get myself properly tested and begin treatment. The clinic runs on a skeleton crew of night nurses during the weekend, and they wouldn't be able to do more than strap me down and sedate me. At least this way, I can start treatment sooner, rather than later. I slip inside my office and unlock one of the file cabinets to pull out a small clear box, stuffed with cotton and a few small blue pearls.

What are those?

All the physicians keep a four-week dose on hand for emergency situations. The only question is, do I take one now and hide out in my office for the next four hours while it runs through my system, or do I take them at home and risk an episode on the way back?

Don't stay here. Smells wrong.

The familiar smells of ammonia and lemon, usually no more than a faint background detail, are filling my nostrils in an inescapable way, like a rag being held to my face. I slip the pills into my pocket, and leave the office, heading back down the hallway. An especially loud beep sounds to my right. In the fluorescents, I see the name on the chart—Stadtler, L. Liam.

They are awake.

Before I can stop myself, I've opened the door and let myself in. Liam is staring at me from his prone position on the bed. Restraints wrap around his wrists, and slip out from under the covers at his feet.

"Doctor Shale," he says with a raspy throat. "How nice to see you."

I walk over to him and raise his head with one hand, holding his water glass with the other. He looks at me as he drinks, eyeing me.

"How are you feeling?"

Trapped.

"Trapped."

"Yes, you had an episode. We brought you here to recover."

"And the cuffs?"

"To keep you safe while you recuperate."

He continues to maintain eye contact. "And how long have I been...recuperating?"

"A little over 18 hours. You'll want to rest for the remainder of the weekend. We've got you on your first dosage, and we want to see how your body reacts to it."

"Hey, if this thing hasn't killed me yet, nothing will." He sounds like he wants it to be a joke, so I smile encouragingly, slipping my own downward spiral behind a mask of invested professionalism.

"Are you in any pain?"

"No, I suspect I have heavy sedatives to thank for that," he jokes again.

"Liam, I want you to know that I appreciate you keeping our appointment yesterday. It's critical for your treatment that you see someone, and I'm glad you showed me what you're dealing with."

That stops his snark. "Do you know? What I'm dealing with?"

"Better than anyone," I admit truthfully.

"Then you know we're both going to be sticking around," he says, and I note the lower tone. Another delusion. And then I stop.

"Liam? Your case appears much more severe than other patients with whom I have worked. What have you been doing the past few years?"

"If I'm honest, Doc? Running. Always running. Nothing has made me want to stay. He keeps me moving."

Brother.

"He?"

"It is safest," he says in that lower tone. "We have been hunted. We needed to escape."

"Why would you think you are being hunted, Liam?"

"Because they don't want to think they don't know everything. I am one of the exceptions to the narrative."

"Slow the Unibomber narrative, Liam. Be straight with me – how long have you been affected?"

"Years."

"And why have you decided to return to treatment? You've been in and out of the system for years. Why come back?"

"I...we...it hurts so much. There's no connection. Either we agree, or we break."

They are breaking.

Within his gaze, I see a black crack, deep as a tar pit. I step back, vaguely excusing myself. The pills beat rhythmically in my pocket as I run for the entrance.

"Adrian!"

I stop, frozen to the spot as I wait to see who's coming through the front door.

It's Evan.

Shit.

I want to keep everyone quiet, collect my thoughts and use the ride home to evaluate and plan. No such luck.

"Why did you run off this morning?"

He missed us.

"I was called in. Emergency."

"You always let me know where you're going."

He cares.

"It was no big deal. I thought you were still asleep."

"And you left your phone at home. What if you'd gotten in an accident?"

I would not let that happen to us.

"I left you the car all fixed."

"And I thank you for that," he says, pausing. Regrouping. I use the silence to try and get three deep breaths in to my lungs. One...two....

Apologize.

"I'm sorry," I blurt out. "I'm sorry I didn't tell you where I was going. I didn't want to leave, but I had no choice."

Yes we did.

Shut up.

"I know your work can keep you busy," he said, drumming his fingers on the steering wheel. I can always tell when Evan is framing a thought in his head, rolling it around till it is polished smooth and perfect. "I just wonder about you, what you're going through. It can't be easy."

"Going through?"

He knows.

"You don't tell me much about what you do. I know, I know," he says preemptively, waving his hand, "doctor-patient confidentiality. I mean, just in general. What kind of toll it must take to figure out what's happening to those people."

"I don't like to bring my work home with me."

Liar.

"Maybe not, but I know it drains you. When I saw you this morning, don't get me wrong, you were way too intent on dusting, but you also looked more...you. Seems like most days you're too tired to cope."

He's not wrong. Even now, with all the stress inside my head, I don't feel tired. It's different than the strung out feeling of the meds. It's almost impossible to describe, but if I didn't know for a fact there was someone else speaking in my head, I would feel normal.

"Was it bad?"

"What?"

"What you went in for, the emergency. Was everything okay?"

I look out the window at the too-bright sun. "I'm not sure."

I can feel Evan's eyes on me as I sit in the armchair, but when I turn to look, he's staring intently at the food cooking on the stovetop.

Talk to him.

He's trying to give me a moment to collect myself, reorient, be alone with my thoughts.

Alone with thoughts?

Yes, shocking as it may be, I used to be all alone in here.

That seems lonely.

Rather peaceful, actually, till today. I look out the window. The skeletal tree branches click in the wind, but the sun is bright, and the sky is that sort of blue that goes on forever. There might be snow coming soon.

Snow.

I remember last time it snowed. I had come home late from work, but Evan had taken the night off and made us hot apple cider, the special mulled kind that we liked to spike with brandy. We'd put it in thermoses and walked outside in the dark quiet, feeling the flakes gather on our eyelashes. We went to the park and wrote messages with our footprints in the thin layer of snow on the tennis courts, and when there was no more snow to write with, we'd just held each other under the halogens.

I want to see it.

Maybe next week.

See it for myself.

Are my memories not enough?

We do not have snow above. Just cold.

The cracks start spreading across my vision. I look down at my hands and see them, like the deep crumbling of an icy lake. Too much pressure, and the ice will break.

Breaking.

I close my eyes and hold my hands to my mouth, trying to remember the feeling of solid ground beneath me. You are not here, you are not real.

I am.

Please, please stop.

I cannot.

I want to cry, but I am afraid what will happen to me if I do.

We can be happy. It is fun. To experience this life. We only get a little time. With you. But it is real.

The voice continues, and for the first time, I realize that it is not my voice. It's very close. It fooled me this long by only speaking in short bursts. But now, I hear that it's different, another female voice, slightly huskier than mine, higher in pitch at the end of her sentences.

We chose you. Your lives. For ours. Until we break.

I keep my eyes closed, even as the cracks seep behind my eyelids. I remember the darkness in Liam's eyes, and the voice that seemed to speak through and for him. How long had I known, in my heart, that these were not mere psychotic breaks? Why did we think that in the first place?

Easy to accept illness. Harder to accept reality.

I feel the pill box pressing against by chest as I curl up tighter. And what is the reality? I don't want to know, but I have to.

We were collected. Within the blackness, light starts to emerge, stars blinking into being within a galaxy. **All parts of one whole.** A star near me flashes, and I feel myself flash in return, light pulsing through my being. The others begin to flash, and I feel us all buoyed up. **Eons we wandered.** The cosmos rush by, planets and asteroids coming into focus and then fading into the void. **Absorbing.** What I see, the other stars see. **Assimilating.** The entirety of the universe, compacted into firing neurons and flashing colors.

And then we found you. We stopped, hovering above a ball of blue spinning in the void.

Humans. So different. Separate, yet strong. Stronger. The world is encircled by a net of thoughts, wishes, prayers, that we are unable to penetrate. We band together, discussing, debating. It is the first debate we've ever had. We don't understand why some of us want to stay, and some of us want to leave. We have never known disagreement.

We splintered. Some of us wanted more. Wanted to know.
We create a vessel to carry us safely through the web of thoughts encircling the globe. Half of us stay behind, to be a lifeline back through the atmosphere. We descend, and upon arrival, attempt communication with the humans we encounters. It fails. We cannot communicate with them. We do not have voices they can hear. So we begin to join with the hosts. But something is wrong.

Some of us. Did not survive the process. Some of us. Break.

Is that what is happening now?

If we are rejected. Too long. We break. We can no longer hear each other as we used to. The connection to those we left behind is lost. We are no longer linked. And our hosts do not understand us.

You are living inside us.

We became part of you.

It's been years. There have been no new cases.

Silence.

Why are you here now?

Silence.

Why did you wait?

I did not wish to understand death. I'm floating in a miasma of screams and whispers, too bright and too dark. I'm eternally drowning in sensations I lack the skills to process. **Forever I waited. Alone. Lost. I did not bond. And the others. Were breaking. I could hear their screams.**

And then I heard you. I had been following another of my kind, in a body that had allowed them more control over him. I would hear snippets I recognized, but I had no way to tell them I was there. Language of any kind was hard to hear, much less understand without the ability to process emotions. These unknown sensations had wrapped tighter and tighter around me. There was no escape.

Then, within a furious confrontation, I heard, felt, the words. **I am here.** A beacon, a pinnacle. I saw you wrapped around the host. **I am here.** In your words, I felt. Finally, I felt something. I felt strength. Anger. Fear. Hope. **I am here.** There was no guarantee it would work. I had been alone so long. You might resist the bonding. We might break.

Then why? Without knowing, without any guarantee of survival, as we work every day to eradicate you, why did you do it?

I can hear laughter. It is beautiful.

You were the first thing to ever divide us. We wanted to know. Why.

I finally open my eyes, and immediately have to shade my gaze in the afternoon sun. I can hear the sizzle of grilled chicken and peppers, and there is a pressure on my shoulder. I turn and blink to make out Evan, his hand on my shoulder. He looks like he's about to say something, rolling his thoughts again, but I put my hand on his, and he leans down to kiss me instead.

"So, how are you today, Greg?"

"Pretty good, doc. Things have been quiet. Calm. I've been enjoying it. Took the wife on a trip up the mountain this past weekend."

"Ah, get in some good time on the slopes then?"

"Not really," he says happily.

I settle the machinery around him like usual, and take my normal seat.

"It's been over three months since your last incident, Greg. Has anything unusual happened since our last session?"

"Nah, doc. Like I said, it's been quiet."

"Do you ever hear that voice anymore?"

"I barely even hear myself think anymore. I try to not hang out in my head so much, just do the exercises you gave me, and focus on the here and now."

I smile. "Then Greg, I am pleased to report that, after three months accident-free, we can officially declare you in remission. Of course, that could change should these symptoms return..." I trail off as he starts crying. "No need for tears, Greg. You should be happy—you did all the heavy lifting to make this happen."

"I'm sorry. I'm not sure why I'm crying, to tell you the truth. I am happy, and sad too, if that makes sense. Like, it's the end of something." He brushes his tears away, laughing. "You know, it's funny. That accident at the park, it changed me. I'd been fighting and fighting for so long, and with Camille gone, I was at a low point. I even thought about...well, about doing a bad, bad thing. And then, that voice just took over, and said that I had to let go, stop worrying, do something crazy, something fun. And I remembered how Camille and I had gone skinny-dipping back when we were kids. Course," he chuckles, "I didn't make it to the lake at the park before the cops were on me. But all the same, it's like I woke up." He finishes cleaning himself up, and gives a sheepish grin. "Bet you're all gonna joke about how I made a mess of myself after I head out, huh?"

"I wouldn't know, Greg. You're my last appointment of the day. I'm heading out myself, on vacation."

"Very nice," he says, and knowingly waggles his eyebrows. "I hope you're bringing someone along to keep you company."

I smile as I draft up his discharge papers, and lead him out to the observation room to fill out the final paperwork with Lisa. I give Greg a congratulatory hug, and wave goodbye to Lisa as

I walk out the front door. Evan's already waiting for me with a second helmet in his hand, bags strapped to the sides of the bike. We kick the last bit of post-winter slush from our boots as we pull out of the parking lot and onto the street. By tomorrow, all evidence of snow will have disappeared, but by then, we'll be on a beach somewhere.

I don't know if I'll like the beach.

Trust me, you will.

It's just so much water. What do we do if the waves carry us out to sea?

Now who's the worrier?

You must be rubbing off on me.

"What are you two talking about back there?" Evan's voice comes in through the helmet mics. Great—I've become as predictable as he is. I give him a pinch and wrap my arms tighter around his waist.

"Just confirming that the beach is a really fun place."

"Oh yeah, we're going to have a great time. We'll play volleyball, drink rum punch, and go for walks at night."

I do like our walks at night.

It'll be wonderful, I promise. We take the ramp to the highway. The sky is a bright blue, without a cloud in sight, and the sun is at our backs.

It's going to be a great day.

BACKGROUND FOR
THE LAST INVADER

What real world conspiracy theory inspired you?
Alien invasion, bodysnatchers, and lizardfolk, mixed with angelic
possession.

What other ramifications do you foresee if it were true?
My hope would be that, though it would be unlikely that
visitors from other worlds share our vision for the future, that
psychologically linking us together would force us both to
compromise and grow through the newly formed relationships.
Also, getting the world to take mental health seriously would be
a great side effect.

What media was crucial to your research?
Honestly, *Venom*. I never really got into the character until
the 2018 movie, which definitely had its problems, but opened
up for me the concept of symbiotic lifeforms. *Steven Universe*
was also influential in the idea of fusion, and the sympathetic
and sympathizing alien. Pairing the concept of beneficial
relationships in nature with more psychological links opened up
a different angle to explore an alien invasion.

What further reading would you recommend?
Anything by Ray Bradbury. As a reader who often finds it
difficult to find an opening into sci-fi, Bradbury's work remains
poignant, thought-provoking, and accessible.

COMPANY POLICY

Tim Lieder

Welcome to Omega Group. This packet serves as your introduction. Omega Group is one of the top consulting firms in North America. You have been chosen from a diverse and highly talented pool of candidates because we feel that you have the Omega Group qualities: determination, ambition, and a willingness to work hard. Once you've perused the materials, please feel free to ask your orientation leader any questions. We are eager to assist your transition.

History

Omega Group began in 1855 when Thomas Eaton opened a small dry goods store in Lawrence, Kansas despite the Missouri/ Kansas border war. Eaton Dry Goods prospered in that turbulent time, ceasing operations only for a short while in 1863 when William Quantrell's raiders killed 67 Lawrence civilians. Thomas survived the raiders by hiding in his basement and allowing them to set fire to his store.

In 1866, Thomas Eaton rebuilt his business and thrived in the post-war economy. By 1871, he had expanded into lady's apparel and hardware. In 1873, his cousin Jethro came up from Mississippi to help manage the business. It was Jethro who introduced him to the Visitors. He had established a relationship with them throughout the war, as they offered him an opportunity to voluntarily assist in research and development.

The Visitors were so impressed with Thomas Eaton's tenacity that they offered him a position in their biomedical division. He refused but countered their request with an offer of full partnership. When Thomas Eaton died in 1903, he had successfully established the first Terran/Visitor partnership in the United States.

Today we are the industry leader in 23 different products and services including sports bras, tennis rackets, and radiology scanners.

Dress Code

All offices are business casual. No jeans, sweatshirts, t-shirts or ripped clothing will be tolerated. Management asks that you do not wear polo shirts to work as they offend the Visitors. Those working in direct contact with Visitors will wear specially designed glasses at all time. These glasses are for your protection and help you to interact with Visitors, as their true appearance may interfere with your ability to conduct your daily work.

In the past, employees have removed the glasses in order to see the Visitors without filtering. While some have managed to function without adverse affects, many have experienced unfortunate reactions including blindness, hallucinations, and depression. Company policy dictates that you wear glasses at all times when in contact with Visitors; therefore your employee health insurance will NOT pay for any medical or psychological conditions that arise from ignoring said policy.

Every second Friday is Casual Friday in which case you may wear jeans but please only wear jeans in good condition. Please do not wear Hawaiian shirts if you have direct contact with Visitors as they find the bright patterns detrimental to their well-being.

Initiation Ceremony

Undoubtedly, you've heard several rumors about the Initiation Ceremony. Please be assured that it's nothing dire. You will not be asked to relinquish your liver. You will not be led into a basement full of candles and forced to kiss a donkey. No one will slap you, hit you, or force you to wear mashed potatoes in your hair. This is a place of business, not a fraternity.

The Initiation Ceremony is confidential and any disclosure of the actual Initiation Ceremony to non-employees is grounds for dismissal. Should you disclose the details, you will be in breach of contract. We will not hesitate to utilize all legal means to recoup any losses that may come from disclosure, including civil suits. Should you prove unable to complete the Initiation Ceremony, you will be asked to leave immediately.

Within the next three weeks, you will be given your company car and you will drive it to a lonely stretch of highway at least ten miles from the nearest city. Once on that road, you will drive back and forth flashing your headlights at passing motorists. When a motorist flashes his or her headlights back at you, you are to pursue them, run them off the road and shoot all passengers in the head. Upon completion, you will call company liaisons who will fly out, confirm the kill, and dispose of all evidence.

Upon confirmation of completion, you will be allowed to keep the company car. It's yours for the duration of your employment at Omega Group.

We recommend that you drive out to a location where you are certain of not knowing anyone. Thus far, we have had no personal mishaps; however, please note that we have a very strict policy against our employees utilizing the Initiation to carry out personal vendettas.

Rules of Conduct

All employees are expected to arrive to their assignments neat, clean, and punctual. Employees are expected to perform their tasks to the best of their ability. Employees are not to conduct personal business on company time. All personal email and internet usage should be restricted to break times.

We strive for a non-hostile workplace and any harassment based on racial, ethnic, or sexual orientation is grounds for dismissal. We take sexual harassment very seriously and we will conduct a thorough investigation into any claim thereof. Sexual harassment is grounds for disciplinary actions, including suspension without pay and dismissal.

Employees are not to refer to the Visitors in a derogatory manner. Any employee using discriminatory terms for the Visitors are subject to immediate dismissal without pay. These terms include but are not limited to: extraterrestrials, ET, alien, alien invaders, Martians, probe buddies, saucer men, bug people, and Cattle Rapers. Please do not pronounce their species name in their native tongue as that feat requires double tongues and mandibles. For your convenience, they have all adopted terrestrial names. Please refer to them as either their terrestrial name or an honorific "Sir" when addressing them.

Non-disclosure Agreement

By accepting employment, you agree to not divulge company secrets, company rules of conduct, corporate methodology, company mission statement, and the existence of certain divisions. Furthermore, you agree that all of your work will belong to Omega Group. Should you violate these terms, you will be subject to legal action, including but not limited to lawsuits, public disclosure of your role in the Initiation Ceremony, and Visitor Tribunal Justice with penalties determined by Visitors.

Please sign and date to confirm that you understand this policy. Again, welcome to Omega Group. We are certain that your time with us will prove mutually beneficial.

BACKGROUND FOR
COMPANY POLICY

What real world conspiracy theory inspired you?
That information is classified.

What other ramifications do you foresee if it were true?
That information is also classified.

What media was crucial to your research?
Our sources and methods are classified.

What further reading would you recommend?
That information is technically classified, although much of it
is open-source.

INDIVIDUALS WITH FEET OF THE EXCEEDINGLY LARGE VARIETY

Michael David Anderson

ONE

Eddie Homme had been lost in the woods for hours. He'd been quite certain he was close to the farm when he slipped away from his cousin Caleb, who had brought him out into this godforsaken wilderness to hunt deer. Eddie might have come out here to hunt, but deer wasn't his intended target.

He'd flown from South Carolina to Oregon with his parents on Tuesday after they learned his aunt Jacinda had passed. In hushed tones upon their arrival, Jacinda's sister-in-law Lizzy revealed the cause of death to be suicide, but no one else wanted to share further details regarding her passing. All Eddie knew was that Caleb's brother Jared found her, and he was neither talking nor taking it well. Eddie was certain if he were to one day find his own mother's lifeless body, no matter how she shuffled off this mortal coil, he wouldn't take it well either.

He'd been stuck at Jacinda and his uncle Robert's house—or the motel, which looked like it was straight out of Twin Peaks— for four days. Eddie thought it a bit odd when Caleb offered to take him hunting, but his cousin told him, "Hunting lets me blow off steam." Then, in a conspiratorial whisper, he added, "Besides, if I spend another damn minute in this house, I'm going to lose my mind, and I think you're not far behind me on that count."

Eddie agreed. The tears of those around him and all the time he'd spent sitting around the kitchen table, listening to stories about Jacinda, mostly from her teenage and college years but also from the past decade while she, Robert, and the boys lived on the west coast, had made him increasingly anxious. He'd never been hunting—hell, he hadn't fired a gun since his hunter safety course in middle school—but he figured anything was better than being stuck with the rest of the family over the weekend. The wake was scheduled for Monday, and Eddie was quite certain the rest of the family would be ready to kill each other by six on Sunday at this rate.

It was on their way out of town, into the vast environs, that Caleb turned the conversation from hunting tips to the nearby marijuana farms. Eddie went from disinterestedly watching the trees pass in an evergreen blur to listening intently in seconds. "Weed farms?" he'd asked.

Caleb smirked. "Yeah. Weed's legal for recreational use here, whether Sourpuss Sessions likes it or not."

"Sourpuss Sessions?"

"The Attorney General?" Caleb asked, his eyebrow raised. "Where have you been? Living under a rock?"

Eddie ignored the jab. He'd seen mention of Sessions on social media, but he routinely unfollowed or blocked people who talked about politics and had therefore avoided as much information regarding politicians as he possibly could. He didn't care, nor did he want to. All politics did, it seemed, was pit people against one another until they were nearly ready to rip their former friends' throats out. I'm nineteen, he'd reasoned. I have the rest of my life to be socially—and politically—conscious.

He'd purposefully ignored that high school students were actively campaigning in the political arena these days, many as a result of school shootings and the subsequent gun debate, about which he'd possessed contradictory feelings.

Caleb shook his head and continued. "Anyway, ever since cannabis became legal for recreational use, pot farms have become abundant. There's one not far from where we'll be hunting. We need to steer clear. The last thing we want is to get busted on farmland, especially out in the crops. We'd likely get shot for trespassing."

Pondering this, Eddie asked, "You really think they'd shoot us?"

"If they thought we were stealing? Definitely."

Eddie carefully composed a mask of utter passiveness, but even as the conversation turned to other things, he thought more and more about the pot farm...and sneaking into the crops, snagging a bit of the product, and sneaking back out.

TWO

Now, Eddie cursed his misfortune. He'd slipped away from Caleb around 12:30 this afternoon. Speaking idly, Caleb told him the approximate direction of the pot farm before Eddie slipped away. He was sure he'd stayed on a mostly eastern track. He wasn't familiar with the woods, but he'd gone for excursions back home quite often. On his excursions in the wilderness, he found he possessed an exceptional knack for not getting lost, even without a compass. Caleb, fortunately, had lent him one. He knew the general way back to the main road, even if he couldn't find the car; from there, it was just a matter of finding help if it came down to it.

His cell phone, with its dying battery and lack of signal, was only good for telling him the time: 4:52. The sun overhead filtered through the canopy of trees, but it was no longer nearly as high in the sky as it had been. Eddie pulled the canteen of water out of his back pocket and sipped from it. As he stowed it away, he became quite certain that, if he didn't either find the pot farm or his way back to Caleb, he might very well spend the night in the woods.

Once he did find the pot farm, he thought he'd have no problem evading the farmers. He doubted Caleb was right when he said they'd probably get shot. Even if they had guns and intended to use them, they'd have to get a good shot, Eddie reasoned. If he disappeared into the trees and kept moving, they couldn't possibly shoot him, could they?

He wished he had a gun of his own—a rifle like his cousin's .308 Winchester, to be more specific—but Caleb only brought the one. Eddie had asked why only the one rifle, and Caleb explained, "Because I only have the one. We'll trade off." Eddie thought his cousin's answer was a crock of shit, but hadn't argued the point.

His stomach grumbled. He extracted a protein bar from his side pocket. It was already open from where he'd munched on it earlier, making it easy for him to take a bite. He'd ration it and the other two he had with him. He'd had a sandwich with Caleb earlier, back at the car, and it was wearing off. He folded the wrapper down, replaced it in his pocket, and continued on.

As Eddie crested a small hill, a familiar pungent scent wafted to him on the breeze. As he cut between two grand fir trees, he discovered a field of crops beyond a high chain link fence topped with razor wire. The crops, of course, were the sort which he sought: bushy stalks of marijuana that looked like trees, towering well over fifteen feet tall.

His mouth dropped open in surprise. He'd begun to doubt he'd ever find the farm, but now that he'd found it, he was giddy with excitement. He balled his fist and pumped it into the air in triumph, grinning. Yes, there was the matter of the fence to worry about, but there was bound to be a way past it.

Eddie descended the hill to the fence, gripped the links, and peered through. Row after row of wondrously green cannabis indica towered before him. He surveyed the field, but couldn't determine how deep the field ran. The stalks towered over one another, each with blooms so thick he couldn't see more than fifteen to twenty feet into the field.

He looked to his left, down the length of the fence, and saw that it ran perhaps the length of a football field before reaching a sudden drop. From there, the fence undoubtedly turned ninety degrees and ran parallel with the rows of crops. To his right, it ran for half that length before the field gave way to the tree line once more. Ten yards in that direction, Eddie saw a slight bulge in the middle of an eight-foot section of fence.

An opening? he wondered. He went in that direction, climbing atop a small boulder halfway there when he couldn't squeeze between it and the fence. From there, he could tell that the bulge was, in fact, due to an opening in the fence: the chain-link had obviously been snipped and pulled aside. The fence had been mostly pulled back into place, but the middle of the opening still gaped.

"Can't have been there too long," he thought aloud. "The farmers would have already found it and fixed it if that were the case."

With a smirk, he climbed down from the boulder, went to the gap in the fence, and pulled it aside enough to slip through. Once inside, he took a deep breath and, savoring the aroma of the plants around him, smiled.

Later, he'd think he should have taken what he'd come for there, at the edge of the field, but his curiosity got the better of him. He wanted to know how far the field extended. He didn't think he'd go far enough to see buildings, if there were any, but he wanted to explore and, perhaps, tempt fate a bit. He entertained a brief fantasy of being spotted and racing through the field, out the fence, and back into the wilderness as he eluded the farmers and whatever firepower they may be packing.

Eddie slipped between two plants into another row of marijuana, then continued deeper into the field. He wandered this way and that, mentally keeping tabs on how far from the opening in the fence he'd strayed, but the deeper he ventured, the more anxious he became. Finally, he stopped at a spire with bud that looked particularly enticing and began stripping some from beneath the fan leaves and stuffing it in his pockets.

Elsewhere among the crops, Eddie thought he heard something move.

He froze, straining to listen. Silence reigned...save for the overhead passage of a plane. Eddie looked up, squinting through the towering plants, and thought the plane might have been a Cessna, but he couldn't be sure; it passed out of sight almost as soon as he spotted it.

Once the drone of the plane faded, he returned his attention to the plant. As he was about to pluck another bud, he heard a grunt. There was no mistaking what he heard—it sounded like an animal, but it seemed as if it had come from something tall, well over his head—and he was acutely aware of the sound of his heart thundering in his ears as it threatened to beat its way out of his chest.

Eyes wide, Eddie leaned to his left to peer past the stalk into the next row, toward where he'd heard the grunt. It was damn close, he thought, only feet away, but at first he saw nothing save for green plants interspersed with a brown stalk. Eddie frowned, thinking he was looking at a stalk that was dying, but the leaves didn't look right. They looked long and ragged, like long, unwashed dog hair.

He followed it down to the ground where he saw something else that didn't sit right with him: the stalk didn't simply protrude from the earth. The plant appeared to dead-end against the earth and bend at an unnatural ninety-degree angle and continue on for at least a foot and a half...and what were those ugly stubs at the end? The stub closest had something hard atop it....

Like a toenail, filthy and encrusted with both dirt and fungus.

Slowly, Eddie looked up, higher than he'd looked before, and found himself face to face with the most grotesque creature he'd ever seen in his life. It was intelligent, hairy, and furious. Its eyes, which looked horrifyingly human, bore into his, and the rictus of its mouth twisted into a feral snarl as it roared at him.

Eddie turned and ran. If he'd thought his heart had been trying to beat out of his chest before, now it was on the verge of shattering his sternum and bursting through his flesh. He was acutely aware of his feet pounding dirt, of the feeling of the plants tearing at him as he plunged from one row to the next, as the beast came for him.

The fence! he thought desperately. Where's the gap? Where is it?

In his panicked frenzy, he'd gotten turned around. He wasn't even sure which way the woods were anymore, let alone the gap in the fence.

As Eddie ran, his right foot plunged into a hole. He was mid-stride, and momentum carried him forward. He didn't feel the pain at first, but he heard the god-awful crack as a bone in his leg snapped a second before his body hit the dirt.

Seconds passed, and he exhaled, blowing dirt from his mouth.

Then the pain engulfed him, and he opened his mouth in a mortified pant. He twisted, turning to look, and saw the horrible protrusion through the leg of his jeans, the spreading blood stain above his boot around his shin. His brain couldn't initially comprehend what he was seeing—in fact, it vehemently denied what it knew to be true—and he could only watch as the blood spread around the unnatural bend in his leg and experience the agony as it emanated from the injury in sickening waves.

The creature had slowed its pursuit. It now stepped through the neighboring stalks and peered down at Eddie, its face tense and attentive as it studied him.

The horror and the agony proved too great for Eddie in that moment. The bile rose in his throat, and as he opened his mouth—to say what, he wasn't sure—he regurgitated, spewing bits of half-digested protein bar and bile onto the dirt beside him.

The creature grunted, turning away from the effusion. Once Eddie had finished, it turned back, and the fury it had once possessed was replaced by distaste. It opened its mouth and said in a deep, broken cadence, "Stoopid keed."

Eddie regarded it with growing astonishment, and stammered, "Y-y-you can speak?"

It rolled its eyes, and in that expression, two terms Eddie's thoughts had been unable to conjure before surfaced: Bigfoot. Sasquatch.

It leaned down toward him, and a stench not unlike that of a wet dog washed over Eddie. "Please!" he cried. He thought he might puke again. "Don't hurt me!"

The sasquatch ignored his plea. It picked Eddie up as if he were a ragdoll, and he screamed as his foot twisted free of the hole in the earth, exacerbating the pain in his shin. Blackness tore in from the edges of his vision, obliterating conscious thought, and Eddie knew nothing for a time.

THREE

When Eddie regained consciousness, the first thing he was acutely aware of was the sensation of being suspended in air, but that couldn't be, not with fluffy pillows in silky smooth cases beneath his head.

His eyes didn't want to open at first. He tried to will his eyelids apart, but they remained insistently closed, as if he'd lost the ability to command his nerves. He groaned deep in his throat, without opening his mouth, and slowly shook his head. Even blind, the room in which he reclined swam and resisted him; it felt like his head moved through air as thick as molasses.

He tilted his head to the right and downward, toward his chest. His mouth hung agape. The tiniest sliver of drool escaped his lips and ran down his chin.

Eddie tried to open his eyes again. This time he managed to do so, but only in gradual increments. The world was bright, and cataclysms of light ripped through the veils of darkness lingering in his vision, driving spikes deep into his optical nerves. It took the work of several minutes before the fog lifted from his vision and he could begin to take in his surroundings, but even then he was forced to wince against the sunlight shining through the window opposite where he lay.

"I was wondering when you'd come around," a voice said to his immediate right. It filled his ears with such force Eddie might have mistaken it for the voice of God minutes ago when he was still clawing his way upward into consciousness. Now he jerked his head to the right, and he felt the damp spot on his shirt from his drool shift against his chest. The sudden movement brought paroxysms of pain, and black spots like explosions of antimatter shimmered across his vision.

A man loomed over him: tall, muscular, with a face featuring chiseled contours both strange and oddly familiar. Eddie couldn't place the familiarity he sensed, not at first, but when he studied the man a few moments longer, he realized the eyes were...

Panic seized him. The eyes belonged to the creature that had chased him through the crops. Eddie tried to sit upright but found he couldn't. His body wouldn't respond. He tried to lift his right arm and found he could only shift it somewhat. He wasn't restrained, but his arm was too heavy for him to lift.

He attempted to speak but found he couldn't at first. He closed his mouth, swallowed, and tried again. What came out was a butchered string of consonants that only vaguely formed the inquiring words, "Do to me?"

The man sighed. "We had to give you a sedative. Something to help with the pain. You suffered a compound fracture and went into shock. We had to do something about that."

Eddie thought of the odd protrusion he'd seen bulging in his jeans, the spot of blood spreading around it, and the horror of it washed over him again. He could imagine the broken bone jutting through his skin, white amidst torn, bloody muscle. A horrific shudder he couldn't repress ran down the length of his spine, leaving him chilled.

Then he thought of the first word the man had said in response to his mangled question. Eyes widening, Eddie managed to ask, "We?"

"Cindy and I," the man replied. Then, realizing Eddie must have no idea who Cindy was, he added, "Cindy's my wife." He laughed then and turned away. Eddie watched him cross the room, grasp the back of a chair, and carry it back to Eddie's side, where he set it and sat down upon it. "You'll have to forgive me. We don't get too many...visitors out here. When we do, they're here for the pot, much like I surmise you were, only they're representatives of the shops and clinics that sell it, unlike yourself."

Eddie said nothing. He only stared.

"I'm sure you have questions," the man said, slapping his hands down on his knees before rising to his feet. "I know I certainly would if I were in your position. So we're going to talk for a spell before we have you for dinner. Cindy's cooking now. Then we'll figure out what to do."

"I saw something out there."

The man smiled. "I know you did. You saw me, son."

That shudder again. This time, Eddie's body succumbed to it, and he trembled.

The man leaned over and patted his shoulder. "There now. There is, of course, an explanation. You're one of the few people who's ever seen one of my kind up close. Seeing me in that state must explain some of the reason why we're normally not found."

Eddie frowned. He stewed on it, considering what he said. "You can change."

The man smiled again, wider this time. "Yes, I can." He began to pace the room, turning this way and that at regular intervals. Eddie imagined he might wear a rut into the floor much like Bugs Bunny had in one of those old Looney Tunes cartoons. "My wife and I both change, as you put it. I've always considered us shapeshifters, or a bit like lycanthropes personally. We grow hair, enlarge, and ultimately shed all the hair when it's time for us to change back. I think of this form, the human form, as our defense mechanism though, because as a species, I don't think we'd survive in the world with how much most people hate other people who aren't like themselves. Oh, it's nice to talk about it!" he relished. "It's rare I get to be so candid about what I am."

"So you're a sasquatch?" Eddie asked, finding his voice. He spoke louder and stronger than he had since he first regained consciousness. He still found it difficult to move his head though, but he was able to track the man's movements all the same. "Bigfoot?"

The man regarded him with an expression not unlike the one a Sphinx may regard an individual: cryptic, unreadable. "You could say that, yes. I've never cared for the terms myself, but we've never had a name for ourselves. At least, not to my knowledge.

"For generations, my family lived in Washington. I moved here with my father after Mt. St. Helens blew. My mother and sister, along with countless others of my kind, were killed in the blast. I can't even begin to tell you how many bodies I saw the national guard take down from Mt. St. Helens in the weeks following the blast, but the government took care of us and relocated us here. My dad was shot by a hunter in the days after 9/11, and it's been me, Cindy, and the kids ever since."

The man sighed, looking down at Eddie. "You're probably wondering why I'm telling you all this."

Eddie held his tongue. The more the man told him, as seemingly innocent as it had all seemed, the more he thought of

The Incredibles and how Syndrome realized at one point in the film that he'd been doing what was referred to as "monologuing." That's what this man that wasn't a man was doing now: monologuing.

"I tell you this so you'll understand that no one knows you're here, and I'll do whatever I can to protect my family. The police will never find you here, nor would they want to. We're protected, you see. When the highest levels of government see you as an asset and they assign you to government-owned land, certain things tend to get overlooked in your favor."

Throughout the man's threat, Eddie's heart rate accelerated. Now he opened his mouth and stammered in a desperate, pleading voice, "Please, just let me go. My cousin is out there in the forest! He knows I've gone missing. Just please get me to a hospital, and I swear I won't say a word to anyone about anything I've seen or heard here."

"Oh, you say that, but that means one drunken night a few years from now, you'll spill the beans about this little pot farm outside of Portland run by a sasquatch, and next thing I know, you and a posse happen to show up at my front gate with shotguns and pitchforks." He scoffed. "I think not."

"They may show up anyway!" Eddie nearly shouted. "How else do you think I found you? Caleb was the one who told me your farm was out here in the first place!"

The man smirked and pulled a phone from his pocket. The screen illuminated and he selected an application on the screen. "Caleb, you say? Gee, would this happen to be him?" He quickly entered the phone's photo gallery and tapped the latest photo. It enlarged to fill the screen, and he turned the phone toward Eddie, whose blood ran instantly cold. The image showed Caleb's slack face, skin pale, one side caked in dried blood. His limbs had been broken and folded in toward his body so he could fit inside a chest freezer. His body rested atop a bed of ice, and his eyes stared vacantly past the camera, seeing nothing.

Eddie exhaled, able only to stare.

"Caleb showed up half an hour after you passed out. He wasn't exactly pleasant, so I was forced to...take care of matters." The man pulled the phone away. As Eddie watched, he deleted the photo from his phone.

"I don't understand," Eddie practically gasped. "You said we'd figure out what to do after we had dinner. Why give me hope if you never had any intention of letting me go?" The man cocked his hand, and after a moment's consideration he laughed and slapped his thigh. "You thought we were going to let you go?!" He laughed even harder. "Oh boy, you thought we were just going to sit down to dinner like nothing happened and then let you go on your merry way afterward? Wow. That's special." He rubbed his eyes and shook his head. "Boy, did you not notice something was missing?"

The question took Eddie aback. He slowly shook his head, unable to comprehend—unable to process—the question at first. Then, gradually, he cast his gaze downward. Perhaps he'd seen before and simply chosen not to acknowledge what his eyes had so clearly recognized. He had looked down when he came to, after all, but he'd hardly been awake. He'd still been fighting through the grogginess into full consciousness. By the time he'd become fully alert, the man had been there, and he'd had Eddie's undivided attention ever since. Eddie had felt numb, and he'd distantly noticed the pain wasn't so immediate, wasn't so overwhelmingly agonizing, as it had been before, but he'd assumed part of that had been the drugs with which this man and his wife had treated him.

A lot of it was still the drugs obviously, but not only that. As he looked down, the full horror of his situation set in when he saw his right leg had been amputated just above the knee. It was now wrapped in bandages, some of which he could see from this angle were bloody.

Eddie looked up as the man's wife, Cindy, entered, and with her an aroma not unlike barbecue wafted into the room. She carried a large serving plate, and upon it was a massive slab of cooked meat shaped suspiciously like a human leg.

"When I said we were going to have you for dinner," the man said as he picked the leg off the plate and bit into a thick, juicy swell of tender calf. He chewed the flesh, and a bit of diluted, red fluid escaped the corner of his mouth and ran down his chin. He swallowed with a smile before he finished his thought: "I meant it."

BACKGROUND FOR
INDIVIDUALS WITH FEET OF THE EXCEEDINGLY LARGE VARIETY

What historical period did you choose and what attracted you to it?
I chose to write in the present because I wanted to establish an event that happened forty years ago and still had relevance, in the details, even now.

What did you change and what do you see the fallout from it to be?
Ultimately, the changes I made to the world were minor. With a story like this, I wanted something small in scope nestled within a larger picture. Does the rest of the world know what's going on? Absolutely not...at least, not on a grand scale, but there is a cover-up and a conspiracy that's lasted forty years at play here.

What texts were crucial to your research?
I perused the internet for some specificity in details. I don't have my notes on the subject anymore, but I think I spent more time researching marijuana plants than I did the eruption at Mt. St. Helens.

What is a good introduction to this period?
The world we live in is as good an introduction as any to this period. I would also brush up on urban legends and the history and supposed lore surrounding Mt. St. Helens for some additional context.

DR. KANG AND
THE FINNISH SEAHORSE

Whitney Petelka

'Furintomaru' Bottom Trawler, Finnish Sea

Tokino the cook was smoking at the fore of the trawler. It had been a long day, and the purple sunset over the gleaming cold waters was glorious.

"Hey, Tokino!" hollered a young sailor in Japanese as he approached.

Tokino nodded at him. "Kimura," he said around his cigarette. "Want a smoke?"

The deck rocked gently beneath them as they smoked, the waves lapping quietly against the bow.

"Good haul today," said Kimura. "Long haul today."

"Mm-hmm."

"It feels like we are fishing nonstop, but we're still not meeting quota."

"Sea is running low," said Tokino.

"What does that mean?"

"Haven't you noticed? Fewer fish in the net every time we bring it up. More boats than I've ever seen. I've been cooking for fishermen on this sea since the eighties and the amount of boats here has tripled in the past five years."

"The ocean doesn't just run out of fish."

"Of course it does. Too many boats here and too many fish on the quota."

"Yeah, well, people keep breeding and people keep eating. What are you gonna do?" Tokino didn't reply. He smoked his cigarette and stared at the waves.

"What's that?" asked Kimura, pointing. Over off the port bow, a dark patch of water swirled about.

"Eh, gotta tell engineering to check for leaks. This is an old boat."

"No, it's a fish, look!" Kimura tossed his cigarette overboard and maneuvered up the railing, pointing. Tokino saw the dark patch of water and the undulating lines, a snaking short-face head coiling under the bow of the anchored ship, felt a dull pit of fear beneath his ribcage. The sinuous dark shape slipped under the hull. It had to be at least twenty meters long.

"We need to move," said Tokino, pulling Kimura from the railing.

A long thrum shivered through the deck, rocking the boat. Kimura looked at Tokino with terrified eyes as other sailors raced, shouting, out of the hold.

"She just twanged the anchor line," said Tokino. He took a last draw on his cigarette and tossed it in an arc over the rail.

A shout from aft decks—"Man overboard! Minoru's overboard!" A small figure in yellow overalls floating on his back, treading water in small motions, staring up at them with terrified eyes.

"Help me," he mouthed. The life preserver landed close by and he grasped it.

"Hurry, heave!" Tokino and Kimura pulled at the rope with the others. Minoru slowly floated towards them. A dark shape blossomed behind him, approaching fast. A low moan went through the crew of men on deck, for despite their efforts, they were still too slow. For a moment there was nothing but Minoru's face and the white life preserver. Then the dark around him split in a wide, toothed maw with a sound like a whale spout. The jaws clamped around Minoru, leaving only the life ring partially sticking out before it plunged back under the waves with a thunderous splash.

There was a sharp snap on the rope, and Tokino dropped the line.

"Let go! Let go!" he yelled, pulling out his knife. The men dropped the rope as it whizzed out of the coil, shooting into the sea under the ship. Tokino hacked at the securing knot, and the frayed end shot over the rail. Then there was nothing but the rocking of the boat as the waves from the breaching creature slapped against the hull.

Lake Champlain Bureau of Cryptozoology, Burlington, VT, United States

"So there's one thing that's been bothering me about my undercover overseas assignment," said Motokun. He and Dr. Kang walked down the long hallway from Boss's office.

"Only one thing bothers you?" said Dr. Kang. "What an ideal existence."

"I know you're in a mood, but I keep forgetting to ask. What is an Icelandic sea monster doing in Finland? I mean, I figure they'd have more problems with the nakki."

"Nakki are easily dealt with. The faxaskrímsli is a 65-foot long, obligate carnivore that breeds once every 50 years," said Dr. Kang. "Breeding produces one fry, which is incubated within the male's brood pouch. After the fry is ejected from the brood pouch it must get as far away from its parent as possible, or be eaten."

"Pregnant dude fish eats its own children, got that from the briefing. Finland's a bit of a swim though, and there's not a huge amount of water in the Gulf of Bothnia. They need massive territories, right? Surely it's not in the Baltic Sea; it'd have been seen by now."

Dr. Kang waited until they were in the elevator.

"Have you actually looked at the maps you have been given? I thought you had been briefed 40 times." She pulled out a packet of papers. "Here, page 43."

"Looks like a map of Norway, Sweden, and Finland to me."

"Have you not read the map? Look for Finnish cities." "Oh," said Motokun, his brow furrowing. "Where is Helsinki on that map?"

"Oh. Estonia? What."

"Yes," said Dr. Kang.

"Why is Finland just a body of water on this map?" He turned the packet upside down, as if it would fix the issue.

"It always was just a body of water," said Dr. Kang.

"So you're saying there's no Finland." Motokun raised both his eyebrows at her.

"Finland, as it appears in the minds of most of the world populace, does not exist. It never did."

"I don't understand."

"In 1915 the Icelandic populace sent a female faxi to the waters north of the Baltic Sea, in order to control the faxi population as it pertains to habitat space around Iceland. In 1921, Japan and Russia forged a secret fishing treaty. It is much more complicated than a simple treaty, but that is a history lesson for another time. For now, you should know that Finland has always been saltwater and the Japanese and Russians control much of it."

"Huh. So that's why they share fishing space with it. Don't the Japanese regulate their own fishing, like with the Pan-Asian Ecoparanormal Coalition or something?"

"You are forgetting what I would consider important parts of your briefing. Due to the closest United Nations landmass being Estonia, the Northern Europe paranormal division requests the reports and does its own investigations. You are merely acting as a cross-check against the field reports from the Japanese and Russian bureaus."

"You got a real way of making me feel important," said Motokun.

"I was not hired for my bedside manner."

'Furintomaru' Bottom Trawler, St. Petersburg Dockyards, Russia

Motokun was trying to act like he'd been on a boat before. The gentle rolling of the deck made him feel ill, and most of his energy was going towards not puking. He tripped over the lip of the captain's office door and caught himself heavily on a chair. Seated behind the desk, the captain cocked his head at his new sailor.

"Fresh fish?" asked a heavily-scarred Japanese man leaning against the wall. Motokun climbed into the chair, breathing hard. He wanted to spew all over the floor.

"Corporate must really be scraping the bottom of the barrel," replied the captain. "Well? Introduce yourself, sailor." He nodded at Motokun.

"W-what?" said Motokun, feeling dumb. Their Japanese was way too quick and regional for him to follow. The captain rolled his eyes and rubbed his stubbly chin.

"What is your name?" asked the scarred man in slow, deliberate Japanese.

"M-Matsuyama. I am from Osaka," said Motokun. The scarred man scoffed and the captain sighed.

"Wonderful. An idiot Osakan who's never been on a boat before," said the captain. "Think it's just a speech impediment, or is he a moron all the way through?"

"Ah, hell, at least he knows how to speak," said the scarred man. "Matsuyama, right? Ever been on a fishing boat before?"

"N-no," said Motokun.

"You'll have sea legs soon enough," said the scarred man. "I am Tokino the cook. You can be my galley boy to start with."

"I want him on nets within the week," said the captain, marking a logbook. "You don't get to have a scullery maid for too long."

"Just let the kid adjust," said Tokino, winking at Motokun. "Even an idiot can learn to fish."

"Get him out of here, then," said the captain, waving in dismissal. "It's your ass if he gets eaten."

"Yes sir," said Tokino with a small incline of his head. He waved at Motokun as he exited. "Come on, Fresh Fish. This isn't a leisure cruise."

Motokun gathered all his guts and did not trip over the doorway on his way out.

The galley of the fishing boat was small but relatively clean. Tokino slapped a chair on his way by. "Sit down," he said.

Motokun sat. "Mister Tokino," he said.

"Just Tokino," replied the cook. He pulled an onion from a drawer and started to dice it.

"T-Tokino. When captain said I will be eaten?" Motokun mentally punched himself for not

taking his early Japanese lessons seriously.

Tokino sighed. "What did you do to be sent here?" he asked.

"What?" said Motokun. "I don't understand." The onion stung his nose.

Tokino scraped a neat pile of diced onion into a container. "Idiot, nobody chooses to work here. This is where Japan sends people it wants to disappear."

"Oh," said Motokun. His vision swam as his eyes brimmed from the onion.

"I'm going to go ahead and assume you were sent out here for being an idiot. See something you weren't supposed to? Say something you weren't supposed to?"

"I am here to make money for my family," said Motokun, wiping at his streaming eyes.

"Sure you are," said Tokino. He wiped his knife and put it away. "No matter. Things are different here. Listen very closely to what I say, and you might survive the week." He leaned back against the counter and crossed his arms.

Motokun blinked and tried to focus through his onion tears.

"The sea wants to kill you," Tokino began. "The sea is not a benevolent goddess. She is a wild and powerful creature who does not care about a few human lives upon her back. The sea is not your friend. It is your life and death."

"O-okay," said Motokun.

"Never forget that," said Tokino. "Do you believe in dragons?"

"Dragons?" said Motokun.

"There is one in the sea here, with us, and it is angry. I do not speak in metaphor. There are many things here that the rest of the world does not understand. If you see a giant shadow in the water, get away from the rail and find something to hold onto."

Motokun felt an uneasy sinking in his gut, not entirely attributed to the rolling of the boat.

'Furintomaru' Bottom Trawler, Finnish Sea

Motokun braced against the gunwale, feeling the spray on his face and the heave in his gut. He felt the ache in his knuckles as his gloves slipped on the wet rope.

"Hold that fast, idiot!" hollered a fisherman on the scale-slick deck, his Japanese deliberately simple and well-enunciated.

"Damn you, I'm trying," Motokun grumbled to himself in English. He choked up on the rope, feeling the weight of hundreds of fish strain against him.

Over and over the handfuls of net, hauling wiggling loads of fish. Endless fish. Endless rope. Endless windburn and a crust of salt at the corners of the eye. A stench that cannot be washed out. Over and over.

"Government work blows," Motokun thought. He heard a cry from one of his shipmates.

Over the unceasing handfuls of rope and net rose a strange dark column, iridescent and streaming with water, up and up forty feet above the dripping deck silhouetted against the sun, all scale and sinew and dark red ragged fins cresting down like a mane.

"What the fu—" said Motokun, and then he was jerked backwards from the net, his aching fingers screeching as they released their grip. The hollering fisherman from before had a wiry arm around Motokun's torso, hauling him away and yelling anew.

"What is it?!" Motokun coughed in Japanese, his boots skidding. The fisherman spun him about and shoved him at the hatch.

"Go below, moron! The dragon is here!" he hollered. The hatch swung open, and the scarred arm of Tokino the cook shot out and hauled Motokun backwards into the stairwell. The last of the deck Motokun saw was the net full of fish they'd worked so hard to bring partially in flopping back over the side. The other fishermen were scrabbling away from the gleaming leviathan, now falling in slow motion towards them. A sound of screeching metal, and the creature hit the deck like a hammer into rotting wood. The entire ship lurched, cracked, and emitted a long groan. Motokun and Tokino were thrown against the opposite wall by the impact, and for many minutes there was nothing but the roaring dark.

Lake Champlain Bureau of Cryptozoology, Burlington, VT, United States

Dr. Kang moved a stack of immaculate files off her workspace and took out her phone. She stared at the screen in deep thought, finger hovering. There was a tap at her open office door.

"Hullo, Doctor?" said the young man with a soft voice. He had a set of goat horns that curled off either side of his head, much like his golden hair.

"Gabriel," said Dr. Kang, swiveling in her chair. "I cannot remember how to call out of the United States without incurring long distance charges. What application do I use?"

He looked confused for a moment, then realization hit. "Right, phoning over the internet. Here, I'll do it."

Dr. Kang handed him her phone. "I appear to have received calls from my junior operative. Please dial him."

The other line rang once before connecting. "Why did you drop my call so many times?" Motokun's voice was strained.

"I could not figure out how to answer," said Dr. Kang. "You are calling on a different application than the one I have become accustomed to."

"Whatever, that's not the point. Here's the point. This sea monster's pulling some real 'Release the Kraken!' stuff up here. Boat's all smashed, people all smashed..." His voice hitched and he stopped.

"You are saying that the faxaskrímsli is attacking the fishing boats?"

"Belly flopped mine. Ate people right up." He took a shaky breath.

"Are you safe? Have you had contact with your handler?"

"Oh, they're here. Some sort of Coast Guard deal all swarmed in to pick up the wreckage when the dragon left. Jesus, it broke the boat in half..."

"It is not a dragon, it is a faxaskrímsli. Are you injured?"

"Nasty concussion, I was out for a couple minutes. My face looks like shit. They won't let me get off this bed."

"Getting up would not be wise. A concussion requires rest; you have bruised your brain."

"That isn't all that's bruised," sighed Motokun.

"If you lost consciousness for any length of time, you should be taken for scans immediately," said Dr. Kang. "Where is the nearest medical center with a Magnetic Resonance Imager?"

"I'm pretty tired and I'm already there, Doc," said Motokun. He yawned. "I'm gonna take a nap now. Here, talk to my handler."

There was the sound of the phone being shuffled over.

"Hello? This is Tarja Prime. Is this Operative Miyamoto's personal physician?" The voice was high and girlish with Italian-flavored English.

"No, I am Doctor Kang," said Dr. Kang.

"Oh, yes, the bureaucrat."

"Among other things," said Dr. Kang. "I hear that my operative is injured and events have escalated."

"Nothing we can't handle," said Tarja Prime. "We will take the appropriate measures in Operative Miyamoto's medical care. I can have copies of his hospital records sent to you."

"You have a faxaskrímsli wrecking Japanese fishing boats around oil rigs in a body of water that is not supposed to exist. This situation will have international repercussions if mishandled. How do you plan to proceed?"

"Dr. Kang, if your input was required to manage a simple cryptid crisis, you would have been brought in on the outset," said Tarja Prime, considerably colder.

"This event would not have been a crisis had your department taken the appropriate measures before the situation reached a critical level. If the faxaskrímsli is targeting fishing boats, it must be starving, and I can only surmise that you have been remiss in your duties. Now my direct junior is injured and there is the possibility of an international incident. Consider me unimpressed," said Dr. Kang, her tone even. "Prepare for my arrival in Helsinki within 48 hours."

"I certainly hope you will bring the magistrate-signed and sealed paperwork required to meddle in this affair."

"I am a bureaucrat," said Dr. Kang. "You will need a lot more than a poor attitude to deter my inquisition. Expect me soon." She ended the call before the other could respond.

Gabriel whistled. "I don't believe I've heard you be so sass!" he said.

"No," said Dr. Kang, staring at her phone's flashing 'Call Ended' screen. "Gabriel, I will require your assistance for the next few hours. I have a number of tickets to book and meetings to arrange, and I do not have the time to wrestle with my own technological ineptitude."

"You ah, you want me to run the phone and computer for you," he said. "Sure thing, but why are you leaving us? We're making great strides here, and I feel like the place is getting back to normal."

Dr. Kang got up from her desk and stretched. Her joints crackled a bit.

"It would seem that my attention is needed elsewhere. It is time for me to meddle on an international scale."

"Playing James Bond with a killer clipboard game," Gabriel chuckled. He sat down in the chair and waggled the computer mouse. "Fine, I'll be your Moneypenny. What do you need me to do?"

Helsinki International Airport, "Finland," Northern Europe
Tarja Prime tapped a manicured foot on the tiled airport floor.

"Debarking was 2 hours and 30 minutes ago. Even with customs, this is obscene. Surely she didn't check a bag."

The driver shifted a sign printed "Dr. Kang" from one white-gloved hand to the other. He said nothing.

"There she is. The nerve of that woman," said Tarja Prime, waving high over their head. Dr. Kang saw them from afar. She, striding with a purpose down the mirrored tile, did not waveback. An antique, black leather doctor's bag was her only luggage. It was hilariously outsized for her small frame, yet she carried it easily.

"Dr. Kang," said Tarja Prime as she approached. "Welcome to Finland."

"Yes, Finland, I'm sure," said Dr. Kang. "Where is the vehicle?" she asked the driver. He led them out to where a gleaming black Mercedes S-class sedan blinked its hazard lights.

"Perhaps you'd care for refreshment? A late lunch? I've got champagne in the rear cabin refrigerator box," said Tarja Prime, waiting for the chauffeur to open the rear door.

"Please spare me the niceties. I have spent a very unpleasant flight and my only desire at this moment is to do what I came here to do." Dr. Kang set her bag down in the roomy footwell with a thump and pulled a crisp official folder from it. She climbed into the Maybach's quilted leather rear seat and handed the stack over to Tarja Prime.

"Oh," said the latter, paging through the impeccable warrants. "I did offer to send a plane for you...when I called you back, you know, after you hung up on me."

The chauffeur shut the door. Dr. Kang buckled up. Tarja Prime did not.

"Private planes are a drain on resources, as well as gross misuse of agency funding. Coach class is the only responsible means of air travel," said Dr. Kang, retrieving the matching quilted leather lumbar pillow from behind her and patting it with derision.

Tarja Prime rolled all six of their eyes.

Room 405, Helsinki Hospital, "Helsinki, Finland," Northern Estonia

"Oh thank God, I'm so bored," said Motokun, trying to sit up from his hospital bed. "Lie down," commanded Dr. Kang.

He groaned. "I feel loads better, honest. My face looks like hell but my head feels fine."

"Darling, we've been over this," said Tarja Prime. "You've got a head injury and you're on an imperial crap-ton of drugs."

"I heard Europe was supposed to be fun," muttered Motokun, settling his head back into the pillow.

A harried nurse appeared with a large medical file. Dr. Kang began to leaf through it and the nurse turned and left without a word, dark braid leaving the clean smell of soap.

"I think you were quite rude to her before, in the hall," said Tarja Prime.

Dr. Kang ignored the statement and tapped a summary report. "No fracturing to the skull, luckily enough. Whiplash and a nasty concussion, mild edema but well-controlled. Contusions and other injuries significant with being thrown against something. Bit of hypothermia from the water, all cleared up now."

"Yes, Operative Miyamoto was quite lucky," said Tarja Prime. They nodded at the adjoining wall. "Another sailor appears to have cushioned most of the impact. Shattered his spine though."

"Who?" asked Motokun. "Tokino the cook?"

"Uhh," said Tarja Prime, consulting their tablet. "Yes. Tokino Hiroshi, 63 years old, crewed on fishing boats in the Finnish Sea for upwards of 40 years."

"You're gonna want to talk to him, if he's conscious," Motokun said to Dr. Kang. "Tell him I said thanks. I'll tell him myself when I'm allowed to move again."

Room 403, Helsinki Hospital

Tokino was awake, but he probably wished he weren't. A cast extended from his chest all the way down past his blanket-covered hips to peek out over his thighs. He was hooked up to all manner of monitors. He rolled his eyes around in his swollen lids to look at his guests, but the complicated neck brace kept him from moving.

"Ah," said a plump Estonian nurse from her corner. "No visitors, no!" Her English was simple.

"Just a moment, while he is awake," said Tarja Prime in Russian. "This is part of the official investigation."

"Five minutes," replied the nurse, crossing her arms. "Do not agitate him, and do not expect clarity. He is under heavy sedation."

"Thank you," said Dr. Kang in Estonian. She pulled a chair over and sat down where Tokino could easily see her.

"Hello, Tokino," said Tarja Prime, swapping over to Japanese. "This is Dr. Kang. She is here to assist with the investigation."

Tokino blinked, and took a slow breath in. "I told him about the dragon," he said. He closed his eyes.

"Who did you tell about the faxaskrímsli?" asked Dr. Kang.

"I told the captain about the dragon," Tokino said. He opened his eyes and stared at Dr. Kang. "Why are the Chinese here?"

"I am American," said Dr. Kang. "You have been fishing in these waters for 40 years. What do you know about the fax...er, the dragon?"

Tokino closed his eyes and appeared to be asleep. After a few seconds, he said, "We are taking too many fish. The dragon is angry because we are taking its food. I told the captain. The dragon has always been here. We are fishing in its waters."

"That will suffice," said Dr. Kang, closing her pen and getting up. "Thank you for your time, Mr. Tokino. I hope you will heal quickly." She nodded at the nurse and left the room with Tarja Prime at her heels.

"The numbers have all been fine," said Tarja Prime in English.

"I sincerely doubt you," said Dr. Kang. "When are the reports arriving?" "Should be in the office when we get there."

"Good. Let us not waste any time."

Conference Room, Kaupungintalo (Helsinki City Hall), Northern Estonia

Tarja Prime stood at the head of the conference table and addressed the group in Japanese. A bevy of diplomats, business-people, and interpreters sat in close quarters, vying for elbow room.

"Infrasound. With a ping unit attached to the keel, we plan to draw the animal away from the fishing area, into the oil rig sector where fishing is prohibited, and then train it to the boundaries with conditioning," Tarja Prime was saying. "I will now field questions."

"Why not just kill it?" asked a Japanese diplomat. "It has already caused a massive amount of damage to personnel and equipment. Who's to say it won't attack the oil rigs?"

"It has enough sentience to recognize that the trawlers are taking its primary food source in the area. Now, there has been some discrepancy with the fishing reports, but relocation of the animal is param..." Tarja Prime trailed off.

A small, businesslike woman standing behind them was having a coughing fit into her clipboard. Tarja Prime turned and smiled, sickly sweet. "Dr. Kang, do you have something to add?"

Dr. Kang glared at Tarja Prime through her cat-eye glasses and stomped up to stand beside them.

She addressed the crowd. "It does not matter whose fault it is for the overfishing; we are all at fault, all the way up the chain of command." She flicked her eyes sideways at Tarja Prime. "As you all know, this location is something of a gray area for regulations. Not all regulation is necessary, but if you plan to harvest fish here for years to come it would behoove you to conserve this area's resources properly."

Translators muttered to their clients. Dr. Kang turned and waved into the corner, where Motokun sat with a laptop. He was wearing a bathrobe over his hospital pajamas. He pressed a button and the overhead projection system displayed a detailed drawing of a monstrous short-faced seahorse with flagging red fins. There was a burst of conversation in the room, and Dr. Kang had to holler a bit to regain control.

"Now, as to the matter of the faxaskrímsli, which is the name of the giant carnivorous seahorse in question, it is not a dragon. It is not a monster. It is a giant seahorse. You can call it a faxi. Stop calling it a dragon."

Tarja Prime tapped her on the shoulder. Dr. Kang cleared her throat before continuing.

"This faxi is on the European Union list of protected archaic animals. It inhabited these waters before any modern international treaties over the Finnish Sea, and it spent almost 100 years without so much as tearing a fishing net. To kill it would bring many old sanctions that govern the sea to pass, and expose this area for what it really is. We all do a good job of keeping it covered these days, but the fact is that one trip-up will be the end of this conspiratorial arrangement."

"What if we relocate the dra—the faxi?" asked a Russian bureaucrat via his interpreter. "Not just to the oil rigs, to another sea entirely."

"This faxi has been moved once already as a juvenile, from Iceland," said Dr. Kang. "Adults of this species do not acclimate well to new seas. Relocation would heighten the chance of discovery and would not address the underlying issue, overfishing."

Without turning, she waved at Motokun. He advanced the presentation slide. A table of numbers and years sprang up, flanked by a climbing line graph.

"I have reviewed the numbers reported for the last 30 years and crossed them with ecological data pulled from coastlines, oil rigs, and independent fishing inspections. The data does not lie. Despite the steady reports coming from the Japanese, Russian, and European regulatory commissions, fishing load has tripled in the past five years. The amount of live adult fish of breeding age is at a 30-year low. As a result, there is not enough population to sustain present fishing habits, and the faxi is forced to find other means of feeding itself."

The room exploded into conversation, with a few pointed fingers and standing angry pronouncements. Tarja Prime waved both arms above the crowd, chirping ineffectually. Dr. Kang waved at Motokun again. He advanced the slide.

A high-resolution photograph popped up. A foundered fishing trawler, barely floating in the shipyard lock where she'd been towed. A massive gouge in her deck split her past the waterline, welded steel torn in shreds, her inner structure exposed like a spread rib cage. Fluids dripped from the cracked boat; an oil-slick puddle oozed about her. The room quieted to a hum.

"Nature loves balance," said Dr. Kang over the crowd. "She will do mad things, violent things to bring that balance back into play." She waved at Motokun.

Images of the sundered fishing boat flipped through on a five-second delay.

"Argue about who is at fault for the numbers later," said Dr. Kang. "We need to act before this feeding pattern becomes a habit."

'FRV Salainen' Fisheries Research Trawler, Finnish Sea

Dr. Kang gripped the rail with sweaty hands and braced against the rocking of the boat.

"You'll get used to it," said Motokun, leaning next to her. "Took me a couple days." His face was still heavily bruised, but no longer swollen.

Dr. Kang hiccupped, groaning.

"Gotta say I'm not thrilled to be back out here, either," said Motokun. "But I feel better because this boat is like, three times bigger than the one that seahorse belly flopped."

"A research vessel with nets up should hold no significance for the faxi."

"So, I kinda zoned out during all the scientific mumbo jumbo before," said Motokun, feeling the breeze ruffle his hair.

Dr. Kang raised her head. The breeze caught her dark bob and fluffed it out around her face. She looked like a seasick dandelion. "What exactly do you not understand?"

"Are we fighting this thing with the power of music?"

"I am not sure how you came to that conclusion," said Dr. Kang. "We are using infrasound to train the faxi to new feeding grounds. Large marine animals like whales use infrasound to communicate, as do lions and elephants on land."

"It's really low, right? Like super bass?"

"That is what the 'infra-' prefix denotes, yes. It is sound below the range of human hearing."

"Aha," said Motokun. "I was right. We're fighting the sea serpent with the power of dubstep."

"Dubstep is not music," said Dr. Kang. She hiccupped.

Tarja Prime appeared out of the hold and joined them at the rail.

"Wonderful news!" they said. "We have reached an accord with the Japanese and the Russians about fishing regulations in these waters. They have agreed to make the switch to pelagic trawling, and we're putting in new checks and balances on the fishing load."

"It is never too late to rework reporting systems," said Dr. Kang. She hiccupped again and leaned her forehead on the railing.

"Oh, you poor dear," said Tarja Prime, patting Dr. Kang's shoulder. "It's very calm out on the waters today."

"I cannot tell if it is ire or bile rising, but I plan to aim it directly at you."

Tarja Prime stepped back. "We should be reaching the target area soon. Shall I fetch you to the dry lab?"

"Yes," said Dr. Kang, turning from her railing. She took Motokun's arm and followed Tarja Prime into the belly of the ship.

Dry Laboratory, 'FRV Salainen'

"So Ted, do certain wubs mean different words to it?" asked Motokun. He peered over Dr. Kang's shoulder. She was, in turn, peering over the shoulder of a balding marine biologist at a computer.

"Be quiet, Motokun," said Dr. Kang.

"No, it's a fair question," said Ted. "In general? Yes, we know what frequencies other faxi use to communicate. Specifically, no. We have a better catalogue of orca and dolphin language based on numbers alone. There are very few female faxi to begin with, and only one small herd of breeding-age males kept in the Icelandic stud. All of our audio samples are from that male herd."

"Using the gentlemen to lure the pretty lady, huh?" said Motokun.

"Ah, yes," said Ted, pulling up a sound file. Long waves hopped across the screen.

"Cool," said Motokun. "So, do you plan to just blast the speakers till she shows up?"

"Basically," said Ted. "Then we've got some tagging and conditioned response worklined up for her."

"Can I push the button when it's time?" asked Motokun.

"Are you a child?" hissed Dr. Kang into his ear.

"Push the button that does what?" asked Ted.

"Starts the giant seahorse Barry White," said Motokun.

Ted chuckled. "Sorry, but you're late on that. We've been playing the frequencies since we hit the spot it attacked the fishing boat, all the way up here into the oil fields."

"Oh, heck," said Motokun. He shivered. "I didn't feel anything."

"It's a very large animal, and its frequencies are very low," said Ted.

"Where is the faxi right now?" asked Dr. Kang.

"It's on sonar," said a tech, snapping her fingers. "I've finally got it on sonar."

"That was fast," said Ted, swiveling around. The sonar screen blinked, showing a huge shape bearing down on their location.

The intercom squawked, "Ted?"

"Yeah," hollered Ted, "Drop it." He pressed a series of buttons on his keyboard. "Stopping the infrasound now, and the wet deck guys have sent a bundle of herring at our girl. Head up top if you wanna see her chomp it."

Main Deck, 'FRV Salainen'

"What if it rams our boat?" whispered Motokun.

"Why would it?" replied Dr. Kang, clutching at the railing. "There's plenty of fish."

A surge of live herring whirled in a large underwater net off the starboard side.

"She slowed!" said Ted, watching the sonar on a portable screen. "'Bout 20 yards off the net now, so I'm pulling it."

There was a clank, and the net retracted empty, leaving the herring in a silvery ball. The sea itself was a calm, dark blue, small wavelets lapping. On the screen, a huge shape was sitting close to the ship.

"Oh, the shadow," breathed Motokun, staring off at the waters. He squeezed Dr. Kang's arm.

She turned. "Stop that, it hurts and makes me feel more nauseous." A huge splash and spout behind them and a smattering of whoops from the crew.

Dr. Kang whirled back around, but only caught sight of the slick, blue-black tail tufted with deep red fins. Even that flicked away under the waves after a second.

"Now you have made me miss the whole thing," Dr. Kang grumbled at Motokun.

Ted cheered. "Great! She hit the fish just as planned, and now she's heading off, but further into the oil fields. We'll probably have to repeat this method a few times, but since the bottom is relatively undisturbed around here she's likely to make the hunting ground switch."

"Will she come back today?" asked Dr. Kang. The screen showed the huge mass moving away from their location.

"I doubt it," said Ted. "We've got some work to do in the area of incident, so we'll be heading back now. Got a tracker on her at least, so we'll be able to see where she is."

"Then our work here is done," said Dr. Kang. She sighed.

"We can stick around for another week, maybe come out again?" said Motokun.

"No," she replied, turning towards the hold. "The deals have been struck and the new procedures have been put into place. Neither of us need to spend more department time here."

"Don't I get time off for this head injury? Workman's comp?" Motokun trotted after her.

"Boss will send you home for two weeks."

"That sounds awesome. I've got my roomies recording Shark Week."

BACKGROUND FOR
DR. KANG AND THE FINNISH SEAHORSE

What real world conspiracy theory inspired you?
I've mixed a classic "sea monster" theory with a modern one, the theory that Finland doesn't actually exist. The internet came up with that ringer.

What other ramifications do you foresee if it were true?
I didn't even touch on the ramifications of an entire nation being absorbed by its neighbors, much less the existence of a sea that only Russia and Japan access. The erasure of the Finnish people has some far-reaching consequences, but I mostly spent time on the Russo-Japanese fishing trade and its repercussions for the environment.

What media was crucial to your research?
The r/finlandConspiracy and r/trueFinlandConspiracy subreddits on Reddit.com were indispensible because they are the actual sources for most of this theory. For the sea monster, I did some research on obscure sea monsters that have been seen this century and found information here: http://skrimsli.is/2013/04/monsters/

What further reading would you recommend?
The aforementioned subreddits are a truly interesting read if only for the great leaps of logic taken by the believers. The Icelandic sea monster museum has an interesting site and is worth a visit if you ever find yourself in Iceland. http://skrimsli.is/

THE GRAYSVILLE TRAIN ROBBERY

Jason J. McCuiston

My guns were loaded that night. I'd debated that with myself for nearly three days. There wasn't supposed to be anybody at the station besides Old Will Tucker and maybe his grandson, the boy helping clean up the little building for the old man. I held no ill will against either of them, hated the idea of somebody getting hurt by accident. I thought maybe we could walk in after the train had left, our faces covered, shouting and waving our guns. Old Will would just give over the goods, and the four of us would be on our way out of town as rich men.

But my cousin Andy convinced me it was better to be loaded for bear. "If what those bigwigs from the company said is true, there's gonna be Pinkertons on that train, Billy," he said. "And if somethin' goes wrong, you can bet your bottom dollar that their irons'll be loaded."

So around midnight on April 21, 1897, I stood in the alley across the muddy street from the Graysville stationhouse, between Rose's Hardware and Keylon's Grocery, a Winchester in my hands and a Colt in my belt; both loaded, more cartridges in my pockets. I chewed a plug of tobacco to stop my teeth chattering from the nerves and the chill. A sudden rain made the spring night unseasonably cold for southeast Tennessee.

Andy was hidden across the way, behind Thurman's barn. The brothers Felix and George Sims both hunkered down on the platform, behind some crated freight that had been offloaded earlier in the day. It had been their idea to pull the robbery, Felix overhearing some loose talk at their mother's roadhouse earlier that week. Some executives from the Dayton Coal & Iron Company let slip that their payroll was going to be late, owing to some special shipment out of Texas delaying the train that picked up the cash in Chattanooga.

I reckon Felix must've been pouring pretty heavy to loosen their lips that much. The payroll shipment was normally kept on a secret, random schedule. But now we knew exactly where and when it'd be coming into town. And they'd also let slip that since it would be arriving in the middle of the night, the local company guards wouldn't be there to pick it up until the next morning. Apparently something about not ruffling their touchy security captain's feathers.

What's more, the company men speculated that the special shipment was from the Corsicana oil field; a down-payment in gold bullion to the Standard Oil Company on the construction of a refinery. Who knows how rumors like that get started, but that's why Andy expected Pinkertons.

Still, it was too good to be true, the perfect window of opportunity. Based on the number of employees in the mines on Graysville Mountain and in the foundry in Dayton, we figured there had to be close to ten or twenty thousand dollars in that strongbox; maybe more, figuring what the executives made.

It was just too big a temptation to resist.

I was nineteen in 1897. A poorly-educated orphan, I kept a still hidden down on Sale Creek with Andy, and worked part-time for Mr. Keylon. Selling shine and running groceries were my only options outside of going into the mountain that killed my daddy. George, Felix, Andy, and I sure weren't the only boys to lose fathers in those mines or in that mill, but we knew what we were planning wasn't some sort of revenge or restitution. It was about simple greed and freedom. The freedom to get out from under the noses of all those folks who looked down on us; the freedom to escape Rhea County once and for all. And if we could use the Dayton Coal & Iron Company's money to do it, so much the better.

I remember looking at my pocket watch when I heard the train's whistle coming up from the south. It was just a few minutes shy of one in the morning. I kept thinking, As long as everybody keeps his head, everything will be fine.

Of course, not everyone did, and it wasn't.

Best I can figure, after the train came to a stop and the freight handlers started tossing the mail and the other cargo off the train and onto the platform, Felix must have gotten itchy. Probably thinking about that rumored gold bullion from Texas. Someone spotted him, maybe one of the men guarding the DC&I strongbox, maybe Old Will or his grandson. All I know is, that's when the shooting started.

By the time Andy and I reached the platform, Felix was stretched out on the wet boards, a neat little hole between his vacant eyes. George was reloading his shotgun in a cloud of smoke. He must have emptied both barrels at close range, catching the two guards and Old Will Tucker in the blast. The freight handlers had clambered back onto the train for cover, and the engineer was making that whistle scream like a banshee.

I didn't see Old Will's grandson. I hoped he was hidden someplace safe.

Andy screamed at George, calling him a fool and a murderer. "Ain't your brother what got killed," George shot back, snapping shut his reloaded weapon. I just stared at the heavy lockbox, surrounded by dead men in the rain.

The train started to roll out, headed toward Dayton. Suddenly the brakes squealed and more steam blasted out from the engine, bringing the iron horse to a sudden stop. That's when I heard that ...howl or whatever it was that I'll never forget for as long as I live. It sounded like a mountain lion's roar, only filled with the buzz of a thousand cicadas.

Except, it was inside my head.

It was dark on that platform. The rainclouds blocked out the moon and stars, and the downpour had put out most of the kerosene lanterns hanging on the posts. There was a dull yellow glow coming through the window of Old Will's office. He'd brought out a lantern to do his paperwork by, and it sat upright on a bench just under the stationhouse's eaves. That was all the light there was, aside from the dim shine of the engine's lamps some hundred feet up the line.

But I know what I saw, and I'll go to my grave swearing it is the God's honest truth.

I heard a shout, then another gunshot from near the engine. I turned that way just in time to see George spin around, a black cloud of blood spurting from his shoulder. The second shot dropped him for good.

More men with guns poured off the train. Men in dark suits and hats. Men with some of the fanciest shooting irons I'd ever see for nearly twenty years. They cut loose on us like we was prize bucks and it was open season. The air was alive with errant lead, flying splinters, and the roar of gunshots.

I'll admit I was scared. Who wouldn't be, getting caught in a crossfire like that? But what terrified me—absolutely unmanned me—was what happened to Andy. And what did it to him.

I'd grabbed some floor and tried to put as much lead back toward the front of the train as possible, hoping to cut a path of escape that way. "Andy!" I hollered over the thunderous gunfire. "Follow me!"

I heard him scream. But there was something in that scream, something more than panic or pain. If you've ever wondered what sound a soul makes when it shatters, well I can tell you. It is the sound of my cousin screaming that night. The last sound he ever made.

Turning, I saw him standing in the guttering light on the platform.

I only saw it for a minute in that hellish gloom. It pounced on Andy and took his head off like you'd flick the lid off a pop bottle. It was no bigger than a child, with shiny grey skin, and a huge head with big black eyes like a giant bug of some kind. Looking back over the years, I reckon it must have taken advantage of our hold-up; must have been trying to do the same thing I was at that moment: find a way out of the mess and escape those men with the fancy guns.

I'm not ashamed to tell you, I think I lost my mind a little, as well as my water. I remember screaming and tearing off into the dark like a scalded dog. It's more than a wonder that I didn't get hit by some of that flying lead. When I got hold of myself, I was a block away, hiding under the front porch of Free Will Baptist. I remember hearing more gunshots and screams, and then the train taking off again in a hurry.

When I screwed up my courage to go back, there was nothing on the platform but puddles of blood being washed away by the rain. No guns, no spent cartridges, no strongbox, and no bodies. Whoever those men in the suits were, they must have wrangled in that monster and cleaned up the mess before getting back on their way.

I didn't wait for the sheriff to show up. I went home, cleaned up a little, packed a bag, then went to Chattanooga and joined the Army. I searched the papers for a week to see if there was any report about the failed train robbery. Nothing, except a small story in the *Chattanooga Times* about Old Will Tucker and his grandson disappearing from the Graysville station. Another blurb mentioned something about the DC&I Company payroll getting dropped in Harriman by mistake. But that was it. Nothing about the shootout, about my friends getting killed. And absolutely nothing about that little monster.

It wasn't until I got to boot camp that I was able to put two and two together. I met a fellow from Texas, a place called Aurora. He showed me a newspaper clipping about his home town, said it was their new claim to fame. I remember breaking out into a cold sweat and shaking like a leaf on a tree when I read "A Windmill Demolishes It" by S.E. Haydon in the *Dallas Morning News* from April 17, 1897—just days before the fracas in Graysville:

About 6 o'clock this morning the early risers of Aurora were astonished at the sudden appearance of the airship which has been sailing through the country...

And then,

The pilot of the ship is supposed to have been the only one on board, and while his remains are badly disfigured, enough of the original has been picked up to show that he was not an inhabitant of this world.

Mr. T.J. Weems, the United States Signal Service officer at this place and an authority on astronomy, gives it as his opinion that he was a native of the planet Mars...

"The pilot wasn't the only one on board," I remember saying when the Texan took the clipping back before I could tear it to pieces. "I've seen the other one."

I got a reputation in the platoon for being the crazy hillbilly after that, but it didn't matter. I knew what the "special shipment" from Texas really was that had delayed the payroll train, and it sure wasn't gold. I finally knew what that monstrous little thing was that killed my cousin, and who those men were with the fancy pistols. It was a captured Martian, and they were government agents. The train was taking a low-profile, roundabout route to bring it back to the bigwigs in Washington, D.C. or some top-secret facility. God only knows what they've done with it...or what it's done with them since it got wherever it was going.

Many years later, I recalled that that rail line runs through what is now Oak Ridge, the Secret City where they built the atomic bomb.

BACKGROUND FOR
THE GRAYSVILLE TRAIN ROBBERY

What historical period did you choose and what attracted you to it?

I chose the end of the 19th century because it really was a time when our society, much like now, was in a great state of flux. New technology and growing industrialization placed those who lived according to the traditional ways of life—in small-town, agricultural centers—at a crossroads whereby they had to venture into the big cities to find factory jobs or risk starvation. This was also the era in which the United States truly began playing at being a world power.

What did you change and what do you see the fallout from it to be?

In *The Graysville Train Robbery,* I propose that the Aurora, Texas UFO Incident was not only real, but also that the U.S. Government got their hands on the ship's pilot. If this were indeed the case, then the widespread boom in technology and advances in scientific research which we witnessed in the late 1940s and early 1950s (following WWII and the 1947 Roswell Incident), would surely have taken place a half century earlier. No doubt this would have had a profound shift in world history from that point onward. Can you imagine jet fighters flying over the trenches of France in 1918?

What texts was crucial to your research?

I drew upon my own experiences in setting the story in the small town where I, my father, and grandfather grew up. I first learned of the Aurora Incident on an episode of the Discovery Channel's *Mysteries at the Museum,* then followed it up by watching other such programs like History's *UFO Hunters* and several videos on YouTube. I found a solid article on Wikipedia giving the pertinent data on the incident, as well as an image of the original newspaper story:

https://en.wikipedia.org/wiki/Aurora,_Texas,_UFO_incident

What further reading would you recommend?
There is an abundance of great fiction about this era in history, but quite a lot of it focuses on Victorian-era England or Gilded-Age American big cities. From Sir Arthur Conan Doyle's and Agatha Christi's famous detective stories to more modern novels like Michael Chrichton's *The Great Train Robbery,* Caleb Carr's *The Alienist,* and Graham Moore's *The Last Days of Night,* there is a wealth of stories that give insight into the end of the 19th century. There are also tales in the Western genre which deal with the dawn of the industrialized and "civilized" world of the 20th century at the expense of the open-range and frontier lifestyle, such as Larry McMurtry's *Lonesome Dove* series.

THE CONSPIRACY BUREAU
James Palmer

Numbers don't lie.

They could be made to conceal the truth, which is how you ended up with $80 hammers and $250 toilet seats. But numbers, in their purest form, don't lie. For that you had to add people. That was why, when Andrew Carmichael, forensic accountant for the firm Costangy and Marler, saw that last line on an otherwise unimpressive expense sheet for one of the myriad government agencies he was tasked with auditing, he leaned back in his chair and knew he was being lied to.

He stared at the figures, clicking through the pages on the digital spreadsheet, then stared some more. But he couldn't make them add up, could not will them into making sense. He ran a hand through his thick curly hair—what his roommate in college had dubbed his tell for when he was conflicted—and glanced around at the busy office, looking for someone else he could show this to, someone who might be able to impart meaning to the numbers that he could not. The office was bustling as usual, and everyone's attention was elsewhere. No one looked at him as he sat at his desk in the far corner reserved for newbies at the firm.

If he worked hard and applied himself, within a year he could have one of those cushy corner offices across the way, with an actual window looking out over the Washington Mall or the

Lincoln Memorial, instead of a stretch of beige cubicle with a Thomas Kinkade *Painter of Light* 2020 Deluxe Wall Calendar taped over it. The calendar had been a gift from his mother. He hated Thomas Kinkade's work, but he really needed a calendar, and so it was taped up there for now, the saccharine view of a cozy cabin in the woods substituting for a locale that Andrew found far more interesting, the hustle and bustle and history of Washington, D.C.

He watched the organized chaos a bit more, feeling chained to his desk, when a familiar face crept out of an office, making a harried beeline for the breakroom and its dwindling supply of Krispy Kreme donuts. It was his third such trip that morning.

Andrew waited until he reemerged, then stood and flagged him down. The man nodded and, carefully secreting his donut beneath a napkin and a worn ledger he kept for just that purpose, came over to Andrew's desk.

"What's up?"

Lloyd Henry was one of the senior forensic accountants, which simply meant that he'd been there only slightly longer than Andrew. But he was funny and gregarious, and could make a spreadsheet get up and dance, so Andrew liked him. More importantly, he knew he could trust him.

"Hey, can you look at something for me?"

Lloyd nodded. "Sure. Whatcha got?"

Andrew tapped over the the correct sheet while Lloyd loomed over him, forgetting for the moment his pilfered donut.

Lloyd's eyes danced over each line item. "Yeah. So?"

"So, there's money in here that isn't accounted for, and I think this Black Bureau line item is the culprit."

Lloyd gave the exasperated sigh of a parent who has just scolded a toddler for the dozenth time for the same transgression. "Look, these government contracts are like this. Don't worry about it. It probably picks up on someone else's ledger, or the fed beancounters made a mistake."

"But there's an address here. In Virginia."

"So?"

"So, I want to check it out. Make sure it's on the up and up."

Lloyd heaved a heavy sigh and looked at he ceiling as if imploring a deity to strike some sense into a recalcitrant child. "Look, we're paid to snoop. But go snooping too deep and you might not like what you find."

"I just want to check this place out. See what's actually at this address."

"It's probably nothing. A billing office, Hell, it could be a derelict building for all we know."

"All the more reason it should be checked out," said Andrew.

Lloyd ran a hand down his face. "All right. I get it. You want to show some initiative for the bosses, climb that ladder."

Andrew suppressed a grin. "Something like that."

"Fine. I'll cover for you, but hurry back. And be careful." Here he lowered his voice to a stage whisper. "Costangy gave a boatload of money to the President's campaign, so if you find something that makes him look bad, you never saw me and we never had this conversation."

"There are so many things that make the President look bad, I'm not sure one more will make any difference."

"I'm not hearing this right now. La la la la," Lloyd singsonged as he grabbed up his donut and ledger and vanished from Andrew's cubicle.

Andrew got out his phone, entered the address into Google Maps, and left the office.

Thanks to the infamous D.C. traffic, it took him three hours to reach his destination, a nondescript brick bunker of a building in a Reston industrial complex that had seen better days. There was no sign on the door, and by the building's layout he judged it was not the kind of place designed to receive visitors. A wave of doubt fell over him, and he wondered what he was doing here. This could be a dummy address for the company's real location. The building might be abandoned. Was he just going to walk up to the door and knock? He had to be crazy coming out here.

He climbed out of the car and walked up the concrete steps to the formidable-looking metal door. There was a rectangle of glass set into the door, and he peered through it. Inside was a dim corridor. Worn, faded carpet covered the floor, and the corridor lead into a room lined with filing cabinets.

There was a dingy metal box set next to the door with a single, faded green button. He pushed it, heard a faint buzz from somewhere within, followed by a muffled squeak he knew to be someone's weight shifting in an office chair. He jumped back from the doorway a respectable distance and tried to appear as if he hadn't been peeking through the window like a burglar casing his next job.

An old man tottered into view and opened the door. He wore a white dress shirt, a stained maroon tie, and brown dress slacks with a mustard stain on the right knee. His shoes were scuffed. Before Andrew could speak he said, "You're early. I thought you weren't coming until tomorrow. Whatever. Get inside."

Before Andrew could protest, he was grabbed by the arm and hauled through the doorway. Next thing he new he was following the old man up the hall toward the distant room he had spied through the glass. They moved past rooms filled with rusty metal filing cabinets, shelves heaped with paperwork, thick, bound ledgers and other office detritus and into the old man's inner sanctum, a slightly larger, similarly appointed room. Against the far wall, beneath a set of shelves threatening to topple over from their loads of papers and files was a modular desk where a computer hummed. In the lefthand corner a television droned, set to some cable news channel, the sound turned down.

"This is it, kid," said the old man proudly. "This is where it all happens."

"Where all what happens?"

The old man turned and stared at Andrew as if he'd just fallen from the sky. "Everything. Dissension. Doubt. Fear. Suspicion. Hate. This is the Conspiracy Bureau after all."

"Mr., I—"

"No names," he said, shooing the question away with a withered hand. "They're very big on that here. That's rule number one. No names. Call me god if you like. No, not the capital G god. I'm more like one of those old gods from long before. Call me Marduk, if you must call me anything at all. Do you know that one? Marduk?"

Andrew, his mouth still open, slowly shook his head.

"Babylonian god of the city. Marduk. I kinda like the name. I've been using it so damn long I've forgotten my own. I traded a Christian name for a Babylonian one. Ain't that somethin'? Anywho, it all sounds really complex, but it isn't. Not once you get the hang of it."

Andrew stared at the old man, this self-proclaimed Marduk, a million questions forming and then dying on his lips. "What do you do here?"

Marduk gave a raspy laugh. "Boy, you really are wet behind the ears aren't ya? I swear, you kids get younger every decade. I guess that's smart though. You'll last longer. Hell, you're not much younger than me, back when I started. Summer of '48, that was. That was some year. That pilot fella, Kenneth Arnold, had just seen what he described as flying saucers over Mt. Ranier the summer before."

"You've worked here since nineteen forty-eight?"

"Oh yeah. A long time, I know. But you grow comfortable in a place, and good at your job. And it's a damn site easier now than it was back in those days, what with the Internet and all. Easy peasy."

"What's easy peasy?"

"Making the conspiracies, of course. You don't think those things just pop out of thin air do ya?"

"Conspiracies? As in conspiracy theories? Well...yeah."

Marduk laughed, tapping one foot on the faded linoleum that covered the floor. "Ha ha. Good answer. Means I've done my job right."

"What job?"

Marduk thrust a wizened index finger in Andrew's face. "Your job, my boy. That is why you're here, isn't it?"

Andrew opened his mouth to speak, a million ideas piling up but going nowhere. He was here for answers. Why not play along? "Well, yeah. Yes. Of course. It's just—they didn't tell me a whole lot about it."

"Yeah, they're like that. But I'll show ya the ropes. Like I said, it's a lot easier than in the old days. Faster."

"What exactly do you do?" said Andrew, still not comprehending.

"You," Marduk corrected, "will look at current events, trends, pop culture, and devise conspiracies. You'll filter these, channel them through the zeitgeist. You'll post them on the Interwebs. You'll leak them to extremist papers, you'll send them to *The Enquirer* and the *Blaze*. You'll spread the virus. You'll sow discord and doubt. Like I said, it's easier than ever, thanks to the Internet.

You should see the memes I've devised. I don't even make them. I pay a bunch of kids online in Amazon cards. I don't even know what the hell an Amazon is."

"I'm afraid I don't understand."

"Weaponized nonsense, my boy. Sowing the seeds of dissension for fun and profit. People need something to believe in, now more than ever. And you're the one what gives it to them. People need to feel in control in a world that is totally out of their control. They need to know that things are going to be all right."

Andrew opened his mouth, closed it.

"The truth is a sucker's game. Nobody wants the truth. The truth is boring. Or too complex. Or too painful. Of course, everybody's different. Some folks feed on fear. It really gets their motors humming. They need to know that everything is out of control, you see. That everything is topsy turvy and there's nothing they can do about it. It makes them feel in control to know that everything is out of control, you see. No sir, we can't be giving people too much hope. That's why I spread the rumors that the Moon landing was faked."

"What?"

Marduk slapped his knee, obviously proud of himself. "Now ain't that a sockdolager? People. Who can figure 'em? It's always been that way, since back when I started. I did all the greats, kid. Aliens visiting the White House. The CIA killing Marilyn Monroe. The CIA offing JFK. The CIA offing...well, anybody to distract from who they were actually killing. Of course, not every one goes as planned. It was no mean feat trying to cover for Tricky Dick, let me tell you. We both know how that turned out."

"But..." Andrew began. "Really? Conspiracy theories? But they're so..."

"Illogical? Internally inconsistent? But see, that's the beauty of them. Some folks take contrary evidence as proof that their pet theory is real."

"But what purpose do they serve?"

Marduk shrugged. "Depends on what you want. Take the hot button issue of climate change for example. Now, our superiors don't want the truth of that getting out, so I spend a lot of my time these days spreading false info about it, about how climate change proponents are just chasing grant money, stuff like that. People want to believe it. They don't want to know that their own actions are making this planet inhospitable. No, that's not the word the superiors used. What was it again? Inimical. Yes. People don't want to believe they are making this world inimical to life."

"This world?" Andrew mouthed.

"I had to look that one up. You know what it means?"

"What?"

"Inimical."

Andrew shook his head.

"It means unfriendly or hostile."

Andrew was beginning to regain some of his composure. "But why would you want to help destroy the planet?"

Marduk swatted away the notion with a wave of his hand. "No one's destroying anything. Only man in his arrogance could think we would destroy this whole planet right along with ourselves. We could all die out tomorrow and this old world would keep right on spinning as if we were never here. No, my boy. We're making it habitable. For them."

He pointed over Andrew's shoulder, and he spun around, startled at the sudden presence of a man and woman wearing black suits and stern expressions, like a sinister Mulder and Scully from *The X-Files*.

"W-who are you?"

"We've moved beyond the expediency of names," said the man. His face looked waxy, his too-perfect brown hair clinging to his head like a helmet. The woman was similar. They looked more like store mannequins than people.

"I'm sorry, my boy," said Marduk from behind him. "I've been having a little fun with you. I know you weren't sent to be my replacement."

Andrew turned so he could both see Marduk and watch the creepy man and woman. "What do you mean?"

"I sent for you," he said with a grandfatherly grin. That was what was so incongruous—so frightening—about all of this. In any other context, Marduk seemed like such a kind, unassuming guy, someone's grandfather feeding pigeons in the park. He didn't belong here, in this department of lies, this secret branch of government that traded in falsehoods.

"I'm sorry, kid. I knew someone would find those incongruities I planted in the balance sheet, and I knew that, sooner or later, someone would come here to see if this place was on the level. So I pretended that I thought you were someone else and gave you the whole spiel. What do you think?"

Andrew blinked at him. "I think you're insane. I think all of this is insane."

He looked around frantically for a camera, thinking he was being punked. Someone was playing an elaborate practical joke on him for one of those banal reality shows. He was being made the butt of someone's cruel joke.

"Now that you know the truth," said the woman. "We cannot allow you to leave."

"What? But I won't tell anyone. Who would believe me? I don't even believe it."

"Mass belief is of no consequence," said the man as he stepped forward. "All it takes is one person. That is how these things work."

The man's face shimmered, started to melt and reform. The woman's face began to shift as well, their noses and mouths stretching into snouts, the lips receding and sprouting sharp teeth. The skin puckered into scales and turned a sickly shade of green.

"Meet our superiors," said Marduk.

Andrew's knees buckled, and he caught himself on a chair, forced himself not to freak out.

"I'm sorry, kid," Marduk said again. "They said if I found a replacement I could leave. I wandered in here myself, back in the day, itching to climb the corporate ladder. Smug and cocksure of the world and my place in it. Trust the government. God's in his heaven, all's right with the world, all of that nonsense. Well that don't mean a tinker's dam in here, son. Everything you know is wrong. And you're the architect."

"What are you?" Andrew asked the lizard people.

"We have gone by many names," said the male.

"The Annunaki," said the female. "The Naga."

"We came here thousands of this planet's years ago," said the male. "And we have been here ever since, guiding humanity toward the inevitable."

"The inevitable?"

"Your planet is almost right for us," said the female. "Our world is dying. And when your industry is through adding the right amount of pollutants, your planet will be hot enough to sustain us."

"What about us?" Andrew said.

"They take care of those who help them," said Marduk, placing a heavy hand on Andrew's shoulder. "It ain't much, but it's something. This was going to happen anyway. At least this way we get to survive."

Andrew squirmed from his grip. "What if I refuse?"

"Then you must be eliminated," said the female. "We do not like taking such action. It is messy and raises too many questions. On the other hand." She flicked her tongue across her teeth. "You humans taste like chicken."

"Jesus." Andrew felt his stomach lurch, but he hadn't eaten, so nothing came out.

"The die is cast," said the male lizard. "Andrew Carmichael, you are the new administrator of the Conspiracy Bureau."

"But I have a life. A job. Family, friends. They'll—"

"Arrangements have already been made," said the female, her tongue flicking from her snout. "This is your job now. You have a new life. A new identity."

The room was spinning. Somehow Andrew made it into a chair before he collapsed. He looked up at Marduk, grinning his paternal grin. Andrew wanted to punch him in the face, but all the strength had gone out of him. He felt like a deflated balloon. He looked around at the mess of papers and filing cabinets and the TV with its numerous news tickers spreading word of violence and bloodshed and peace talks and protests and wildfires and hurricanes and technological wonders and all manner of very real things it was now his job to distract them from.

When the room stopped spinning, Andrew realized that in a sick way he had what he wanted. His ambition had driven him out here to Reston to an old building where the most horrible secret in the world was kept. He was still pondering the implications as the lizard man and lizard women led Marduk from the room, urging him ahead of them as they opened their jaws wide.

BACKGROUND FOR
THE CONSPIRACY BUREAU

What historical period did you use and what attracted you to it?
I chose the current day for my historical period, because conspiracy theories are bigger than ever, and the climate change debate is a hot button topic.

What did you change and what do you see the fallout from it today?
I kept everything the same, i.e. climate change is real and there are conspiracy theories trying to disprove it, but the reason for the conspiracies is to stop us from actually doing anything about climate change because another popular conspiracy—lizard people—are real and guiding humanity to create a hothouse Earth so that they can colonize it and take over.

What texts were crucial to your research?
I am actually more interested in why people buy into conspiracy theories more than the theories themselves, and was helped greatly by the *Scientific American* article "People Drawn to Conspiracy Theories Share a Cluster of Psychological Features" (https://www.scientificamerican.com/article/people-drawn-to-conspiracy-theories-share-a-cluster-of-psychological-features/). Some important books on the subject include *Suspicious Minds: Why We Believe in Conspiracy Theories by Rob Brotherton,* and Michael Shermer's *Why We Believe Weird Things* and *The Believing Brain: From Ghosts to Gods to Politics and Conspiracies—How We Construct Beliefs and Reinforce Them as Truths.*

What is a good introduction to this period?
Since this is the modern day, one need look no further than out their window or almost any news channel.

FIRST RESPONDERS

William Thomas Maxwell

Clifton's Cafeteria
648 S. Broadway
Downtown Los Angeles, CA
Source: cellphone, video, lo-res capture
Note: Source unaware of significance of capture. Terminated at |REDACTED| on Dec |REDACTED|. Cellphone contents downloaded to mainframe at |REDACTED| and cloud backup erased.

"...have to admit. I didn't expect to see you here, or, honestly at all." The speaker was a plump man, squashed face with a perpetual smirk and squinting eyes used to make people feel uncomfortable. He was dressed in a suit that belonged to the seventies, sporting a cravat which made the whole ensemble deliberately anachronistic at best.

The person seated at the table was much more modern. Casual white shirt. Hair up in hipster mode, well-groomed mustache. Tony Stark in casual mode. He waved his fork at the other man. "You remember when they used to let folks eat here for free?"

The older man took a seat. "That was never my thing, Jack."

The younger man took a bite, chewed with obvious relish. "No Jack Parsons here, Ronald. Just John Whiteside."

"Who was supposed to have died almost seventy years ago."

"Says the man proclaimed dead in the mid-80s. You're looking pretty good for a corpse."

"Plastic surgery and healthy living. You, on the other hand, were blown up. Botched attempt at Aleister Crowley's immortality spell, or so they say. Are you saying it worked?"

Parsons waved his fork at his face. "Isn't this proof?"

"Am I supposed to guess why you brought me here?"

Parsons smiled. "Well you did steal my girlfriend. And a fair chunk of my money."

"That was more than half a century ago."

"Can't a man bear a grudge?" Parsons waved for Ron to sit. "Or just be nostalgic?"

Ron took a seat and motioned for the waiter. "If you wanted me for a grudge, why didn't you approach me when I had money?" He ordered a drink.

"What...from your little cult of personality?" Parsons grinned. "How would that be fair?"

Ron sighed. "You're not going to shake me down. And you're not here because of my world-spanning and very popular religion. Just put the cards on the table, Jack."

Parsons popped another bite of food into his mouth and chewed thoughtfully, glaring at Ron the whole time.

Finally Ron crossed his arms and glared back until the waiter delivered the drink.

"I know you stole it."

The words hit hard. "Stole what?"

Parsons practically threw his fork onto his plate. "You know that's why I had to 'die', right? I thought I lost it in the Babalon Working. You do remember that, right? All the lights and the weirdness and the sex and the drugs and I figured I'd lost it. And in 1952, in some random, stupid, inventory, the folks I took it from figured out it was missing."

Ron tersely acknowledged the mutual memory with a gesture. "You never told me where you got it from. What did you call in it Liber 49? That was that silly text you wrote, yes? 'Finishing Aleister Crowley's work.' You called it the Air Dagger. Why didn't you tell people it's real name?"

"Where's the paraperehelion, Ronald?"

Ron leaned forward, pressing his palms onto the table. "Where did you get it from, Jack?"

Parsons frowned. "I didn't even know you had it until, oh, about the mid-1970s. I picked up one of your books, your 'secret books' from an OT six I was seeing." Parsons looked away, picked at his teeth for a moment. "I recognized Xenu."

Ron let out a hiss in shock. "You 'recognized' Xenu? How it that possible?"

"It's a stupid transliteration—yours is—of what we think was the name of the Ship."

Ron shook his head in confusion, a thousand questions bouncing around at once. "What ship?"

Parsons templed his fingers in front of him. "In the interest of expediting this, if I tell you what the Ship is, will you tell me where the paraperehelion is?"

Ron shifted uncomfortably in his seat. "That might be an arrangement I'd be amenable to."

Parsons leaned across the table and put his hand on Ron's arm in a gesture meant to be friendly. "No need to be so tense, Ronald. We're just two old friends, reminiscing over old times, right?"

Ron couldn't help but react to what he saw as a predatory smile. "Sure." He pulled his arm back.

"Remember the Battle of Los Angeles?"

"No. I moved to L.A. after the war."

"Ah. February, 1942, World War II. Our boys were worried about Japan coming ashore, so when the navy warns them they might see action in about, oh, ten hours, they're ready. This massive triangle-shaped object appears off Long Beach and later Santa Monica and they open up on it."

"You're telling me that was a real spaceship."

"Extra-dimensional ship is probably a better descriptor but you know how it goes when people try to sort out the unknown. Press reported it as 'weather balloon', 'frayed nerves', etc. The truth is the artillery fire damaged it and the thing ended up doing a header into the Santa Catalina Channel, sinking to a depth of about 2,000 feet."

"What was your involvement with it?"

"Jack Parsons, brilliant boy out of Caltech. Out-of-the-box thinker. Of course they were going to call me in. We recovered it—took a while, though—and then moved it over to the western edge of the San Fernando Valley, just north of L.A. proper. Put up the 'Santa Susana Field Laboratory' and got to work. And you want to know the weird part?" Parsons grinned. "This thing, this amazing thing. It wasn't like anything you've ever seen. It was grown or growing or alive or not. It was amazing. It affected everyone who touched it, including me."

Ron looked appalled. "And you just...decided to take a piece out to a ritual?"

"Look, the paraperehelion responded to thought. That's what I was pushing, but they wouldn't believe me! So, I knew I had to go outside the box. Take it to a place where thought was precise, where it was controlled. To a ritual."

"I was a part of an experiment?"

"Oh, it was glorious! Don't you remember? The winds coming up? The shadow people? The voices?"

"I remember being terrified."

"That didn't stop you from stealing it."

Ron turned away, took a deep breath, then matched Parsons' gaze. "No, it didn't."

Parsons' expression betrayed a momentary flash of validation. "Where is it now?"

"Was that the reason I started having the dreams?"

Parsons waved it off. "Just a side effect, at best. I got that from reading your books."

Ron felt a flash of anger. "Those books were very successful."

"To the gullible, maybe."

With that, the brief anger took root. "Millions have taken faith in my words." Ron growled. "And what better answers do you have?"

Parsons leaned back, stroked his mustache. He didn't answer.

"And!" Ron pushed forward, emphasizing the point. "And I used it better than the Babalon Working. I summoned a whole fleet of those...those ships in Topanga Canyon."

It was Parsons' turn to be shocked. "You did that? Jesus, Ron, that fleet melted four of the ten nuclear reactors used to contain the Ship! We barely managed to hang on to it."

That caused an uncomfortable silence. Ron's response was almost inaudible. "Oh. I...I'm sorry."

"Please tell me you didn't use it again."

"'92. Topanga Canyon again. Technically, I was considered dead at the time. I just wanted to see if I imagined it correctly or if it was the drugs. I mean...we did do a lot of drugs back then. In my defense, though, I know your laboratory was closed. Contamination of the land, or something. Nothing happened."

Parsons frowned. "1994. The Northridge earthquake. They started appearing in 1992 and they left after the earthquake, which, not so coincidentally, cracked open the structures that used to hold the Ship. Thankfully, we'd moved it by then." Parsons flexed his hands. "So now you know." He paused. "Where's the paraperehelion, Ronald?"

"That's a complicated answer."

"It's a complicated situation, Ronald. You want to know what our surveillance after the quake told us?"

Ron shook his head.

"The things that showed up; they didn't act like colonizers or invaders or explorers. They acted more like 'first responders'. We think it was a planned rescue mission."

"That's good, right?"

"If you don't count Aliso Canyon. 2015. Natural gas storage facility up in the hills above the San Fernando Valley. The aliens drilled into it and released about 100,000 tons of methane into the local atmosphere, trying to change it. Like giving oxygen bottles to people trapped in a cave. That led me to figuring the whole thing out. The final piece. The paraperehelion is the Ship's distress beacon. It's calling them." Parsons made sure to emphasis his words. "Which is why. We. Need. It. Back."

Ron tapped his fingers on the table. "That might be a problem." Parsons didn't even bother hiding an expression of hostility. "I didn't use the paraperehelion in '92. I used a copy. Sort of." Ron cut Parsons off before he could respond. "A piece of it. A large piece I had grown. I had some people, brilliant people working on it, nurturing it. I had the money to do it. The time. It's the basis for the technology in all our meters."

Parsons look confused. "Meters?" Then he straightened up, with a look of horror. "The meters you use to read people? To get them into your religion?"

"In at least two generations of our most popular model. The paraperehelion kept growing and we didn't know what to do with it, so we'd break off pieces and put them in the meters. We found out that in about 20% of our users, it gave them dreams, and made them suggestible."

Parsons slammed his forehead with his palm. "Oh, you idiot. Oh you brilliant, enormous idiot." Parsons seemed to collapse in a fit. It took a moment for Ron to realize it was hysterical laughter.

"What's so funny?"

Parsons wiped off tears. "You just ended the world. You and your silly dreams of being a messiah just ended everything."

"What are you talking about?"

"These things, these aliens...these first responders...they are smart. By this time, they've figured out that what's between them and rescuing their companions is us."

"So?"

"Ever read the paper? All those asteroids? All those near misses?"

Ron went pale. "Yeah..."

"Well, that's them." Parsons snarled. "They've been throwing asteroids at us for about a year now. Testing out their target system, their precision. The paraperehelion: it's thought powered. Every place they pick up a signal from it? That's where they think a survivor is. A survivor who can't be rescued until they clear out the only obstacles consistently in their way. Us."

"Oh god."

"And all of the meters you made?" Parsons' smile was bared teeth with little humor. "With pieces of the beacon? For your world-spanning religion"

"All over the world." Ron looked like he was going to pass out.

Parsons stood up and threw his wallet down on the table. "Exactly."

Notes: Recording ends as subject gets violent ill. Stress-induced. Cell service is interrupted by on-site operatives before external contact can be made.

SUBJECT PARSONS: Recovered.

SUBJECT HUBBARD: Recovered.

FILE CLASSIFICATION: EYES ONLY

FILE ENDS

BACKGROUND FOR
FIRST RESPONDERS

What real world conspiracy theory inspired you?

It was more a set of weird occurrences than conspiracies that
inspired me. The Battle for Los Angeles was a real event that
happened during World War II and while it was labeled later as
an example of "mass panic", the people interviewed and involved
at the time certainly gave convincing reports that they shot at
something more than flares, weather balloons, or any of the other
stories the Armed Forces put out. There were veterans of World
War I involved too, so definitely some expertise there.

The Babalon Working was another well-chronicled event involv-
ing a rocket scientist (Jack Parsons), L. Ron Hubbard, and the
wickedest man alive (Aleister Crowley). Now whether you believe
the eyewitnesses who saw the Babalon Working in progress,
that's another story.

UFO bases off the coast of Los Angeles and UFOs in Topanga
have long been the chatter among the locals, but the books about
them are mostly hype...unless you believe there is a shadowy
worldwide conspiracy covering it up.

The Santa Susana Field Laboratory and Aliso Canyon were real
conspiracies, coverups for shoddy engineering or insane waste
disposal practices. Because of SSFL's connection to NASA, it's
also been the occasional target of "the government was testing
alien stuff here" but it's never maintained a popularity level like
Area 51.

What other ramifications do you foresee if it were true?
If there used to be a hub of alien research in Los Angeles, which
given its crucial position in the aerospace industry would be
logical, I'd expect usable technology to spread up to Silicon
Valley, where the tech could be safely disseminated among the
population. Which means that if there was something dangerous
about that technology, it would ultimately affect Southern
California first, then the world.

What media was crucial to your research?
The Battle of Los Angeles (weather balloons):

> history.com/news/world-war-iis-bizarre-battle-of-los-
> angeles huffingtonpost.com/jason-apuzzo/the-time-a-ufo-
> invaded-lo_b_6749734.html
> The Babalon Working (Jack Parsons & L. Ron Hubbard were
> both crazy & on drugs)
> parareligion.ch/dplanet/staley/staley11.htm
> sacred-texts.com/oto/lib49.htm

The UFO base off Catalina (spotted on Google Earth, natural
geological plate formation):

> huffingtonpost.com/2014/06/19/malibu-underwater-alien-
> base_n_5493186.html
> prestondennett.weebly.com/undersea-ufo-base.html

UFO sightings in Topanga (drugs, canyons, lights from various
aircraft and Venus):

> weirdus.com/states/california/unexplained_phenomena/
> ufos_topanga_canyon/index.php

Preston Dennett was a busy guy; he wrote a book on the
Catalina UFO base as well as the Topanga sightings.

unexplained-mysteries.com/forum/topic/196234-the-topanga-canyon-ufo-incidents/

The Rocketdyne Super Fund site/nuclear meltdown ('alien weapons program' actually just nutty scientists not knowing how toxic their stuff was)

rense.com/ufo/rocketd.htm
centerforhealthjournalism.org/2013/08/08/%E2%80%9C-santa-susana-field-laboratory-controversy-introduction-santa-susana-field-laboratory%E2%80%9D

Aliso Canyon (government-affiliate didn't want to replace safety pipes)

porterranchlawsuit.com/the-aliso-canyon-blowout-a-tale-of-corporate-obliviousness/
latimes.com/opinion/op-ed/la-oe-michanowicz-aliso-canyon-gas-leak-20180514-story.html

What further reading would you recommend?
For the occult side of Los Angeles, go research Jack Parsons and the Ordo Templi Orientis. For UFOs? Material on the Battle of Los Angeles is often a lot of fun to dive into.

THE COUNTRY DOCTOR

James Dorr

Dr. Ramson wasn't a very good role model, Sally Akers, his nurse, admitted. But then, she probably wasn't that top notch a nurse herself, or she wouldn't still be working for him at his tiny practice, out in the sticks, serving the remnants of what once had been a thriving northern New Mexico farm town. New people didn't move into such places, though, not since the better jobs had relocated into the cities, nor did such towns offer much to retain their own young people anymore. Just their old ones, set in their ways, like Dr. Ramson.

Dr. Ramson did not hold with new ideas, grumbling all the way to the county hospital, for instance, when, once a year, he attended the seminars that the state medical board required. "What's the point?" he would say. "Nobody here gets any of those newfangled diseases, and, if someone did, I wouldn't have the stuff here to treat them. I'd just have to send them to the county seat to the hospital anyway."

Sally would cluck. "But at least now you'd recognize what it was they had."

Ramson would snort back, "So?"

"So you would know when to call out the ambulance to get them to the county hospital. Not just take their temperature one more time, give them some antibiotics or something, maybe a painkiller—rack up a bill for them—then send them home to bed."

"At least, then, the bill is here." Dr. Ramson would shake his head at that. "The point isn't even that we're learning medicine, not that the old ways aren't still the best for a practice like this. Mostly it's just making new regulations, nit-picking little things, to make us send patients to the city. More paperwork to do when we do treat them here. Either way, more expense..."

Dr. Ramson liked to cut expenses.

Dr. Ramson liked to cut corners. His office was on the first floor of his own home, not an unusual thing for a country practice like his was. He bought supplies wholesale, from cut-rate sources, like the rubber gloves the state board of health now required that he wear when he examined patients, even if, after just a glance or two, he could usually already tell when most of them didn't have anything catching. Nothing that he would get.

"That's the trouble," he'd grumble at Sally. "Good doctoring's mostly a matter of instinct, that and experience, not a bunch of fancy tests that you have to send out to some lab to have analyzed. They don't tell you anything after you get 'em back, not most of the time, but you have to bill your patients anyhow—getting more lip from them—sending most of that money out too so there's that much less to keep for your own services. Then, when you've done all that, filling the forms out for the county board of health here, so they'll know what you did. Then more forms for the state..."

Never mind that it was actually Sally who filled these government forms out, she and Becky, the high school part-timer who helped in the office. The point was the same: Dr. Ramson was not very good about regulations.

The doctor did what was required. That was all. He had to do that much because the state board would inspect his practice from time to time, as it would other doctors' as well. It would make sure he did use rubber gloves, and, when he was done with them, dispose of them in appropriate "Biohazard" containers, bright orange bags that received blood samples and urine-test bottles and anything else potentially septic—sputum and pus, even wiped up vomit—which, every third Friday, the county hospital would pick up for proper disposal.

"Like I can't dispose of this stuff myself," he would say.

"That's what the rules are," Sally would answer. "I fill the forms out and that's what it says on them. And if you should have any extra bags some month, more than will fit in the lidded trash cans you're supposed to keep them in until they're full, then we're supposed to call the hospital to send their truck out for an extra pickup."

"And pay them extra too?"

"And pay them extra," she would answer. "But it's only a few more dollars, Doctor. And fill more forms, too, though I'm the one who fills the forms out. I'll even call the hospital for you..."

It was a point of contention between them. The previous month there had been a major accident on the highway, a truck and two cars, both with children in them, and, his office being closest to the site, the state police had brought those of the victims that could be moved to him. These ended up at the county hospital anyway afterwards, after he'd given emergency first aid—and Nurse Akers filled more forms—but the next morning, after they'd cleaned the blood and whatever else from the exam room, and cleaned the equipment too, putting the cloths and paper liners and tissues and gloves and whatever else in the bright orange bags, Dr. Ramson just tied them off as they became full and shoved them into his front hall closet.

"The closet I hang my coat in, Doctor," Sally protested.

The doctor shrugged. "It's still mostly just rubber gloves, Nurse," he said. "Anyway, it'll be only a week before the hospital truck comes by on its regular rounds. And these patients weren't sick, not in the sense they had something infectious—they were just here for lacerations, granted some of them pretty ugly. That and two broken bones."

"How do you know what they had or didn't have, Doctor?" Sally persisted. "You didn't diagnose them for diseases, just bandaged their cuts, like you say, and splinted two fractures. Granted, that seemed to be all that was wrong, but let me at least call the hospital anyway to ask if anything else showed up afterwards, when they did their tests..."

"And just have more paperwork asking us why we're so curious to know." Dr. Ramson scowled. "And I'm the one who has to check over what you've filled out on those forms, Sally, before I can sign them. You know that."

He closed the closet door—five distended bags had been stuffed inside by the time they were done, pushed into a corner. "Anyway," he added, "I keep my golf clubs in there too. If anything were wrong, I wouldn't do that, would I?"

Sally let it go. Country ways were country ways, she thought. Things were done in ways sometimes that would appall someone from the city, and state license board members were, for the most part, from the city. It was best, sometimes, just to keep things quiet.

She made her own accommodation, leaving her coat in her car those mornings when she came to work knowing that more of the filled biohazard bags were in the closet. This would often be in the fall, during hunting season, though sometimes in summer too, when Dr. Ramson got his share of gunshot-wound patients. He often suggested these pay him in cash when he'd cleaned out the pellets—or else accept a receipt for a general physical checkup —in order to avoid the extra paperwork firearms incidents would require, and then the next week, or two, or three later, when the hospital van finally came by, Dr. Ramson would carry the stored bags out to the truck himself under the pretext of helping the driver, so no one would know they hadn't just then been filled.

And she'd spray the closet with disinfectant, then let it air out till the following morning, before she'd start hanging her coat in there once again, because she didn't trust Dr. Ramson. At least she did not trust him entirely, knowing he sometimes cut too many corners.

Then one hot summer night, the kind when people drove fast on the highway, Sally received an emergency call from Dr. Ramson. Another crash? she thought. She drove to the office under a breezeless, clear, star-speckled sky through an almost deserted main street of town—almost too deserted—and pulled in behind Dr. Ramson's house, in the lot for employees, noting another large vehicle next to hers, painted in khaki.

Military? she wondered. This wasn't the southern part of the state that teemed with military personnel, what with White Sands and the other bases. Some that had no names. Still, she supposed, there were always convoys, some that came north on Interstate 25 heading into Colorado—the Air Force Academy— and they drove fast too.

She almost turned back, still, when Dr. Ramson met her at the door, flanked by two men in combat fatigues. "Nurse Akers," he said, "this is a little bit different from most of the cases we get. These men'll want you to sign a form swearing you'll keep anything that happens tonight a secret. After that, though, they'll just wait in the waiting room, stay out of the way until we're finished..."

Sally almost laughed. "You mean more forms to fill?"

"Hopefully just that one. This is kind of a federal thing—it's being kept secret from the state and the county too."

Sally shrugged. "You mean like it's some important general?" she asked, half joking. "Someone they don't want the word to be out on, because of some national security thing?"

"Sort of," Dr. Ramson answered. But he was not smiling and Sally realized why when he led her into the examination room, after she'd put on a surgical mask and rubber gloves, and closed the door.

There, stretched on the table, was the naked form of something that was not of this planet.

"It's true then?" Sally asked, giving its almost human appearance a preliminary appraisal, noting the size of its head and features, large in proportion to its body. Noting its skin, of a pearl-gray color, its four double-jointed fingers on each hand. "Roswell and all that stuff—it's not just a story for tourists? There really are aliens?"

The doctor frowned. "I don't know, Sally. That is, we can see this. But tomorrow morning, we're supposed to forget that it ever even existed. That it was ever here. And we are not supposed to speculate, that's what those men just outside the door said and I, for one, am going to obey them. All we need to know is this, that this...patient had been riding in a truck when, uh, he keeled over. He made some funny sounds, then hit the floor, and they think that maybe he broke something. Or that maybe something was broken from before, from when they first found him, but it just got worse. Anyway they want us to check him, give him emergency first aid, whatever, take a few blood and urine samples. Try and figure out if there's anything really wrong, or if it's just that he's fainted or something. In other words, pretty much what we do normally when the state police bring something in to us, just get things stable enough for the hospital—or in this case, the military's specialists, I suppose—to take over."

"And to keep our mouths shut afterwards," Sally said. Just like the gunshot-wound cases, she thought, that came up every autumn. Or like the biological waste bags that, when they were full, Dr. Ramson concealed in the closet. She wouldn't touch them —that was the other accommodation the doctor let her make. But she agreed, as he put it to her, that "it wouldn't do to let our patients see them out in the open."

And so, when this night was finally ended, the "patient" at least appearing to breathe a bit more steadily—anyway, back on the government truck and out of their hands, heading to wherever it was its guards were taking it—Sally assisted in cleaning the room up, filling more orange bags, figuratively turning her head the other way as Dr. Ramson pushed them in the closet, shoving the one or two already there farther back in the corner. Straining this time to shut the door on them—six bags full this time.

"Like the damn thing crapped all over the table," the doctor muttered. "Like some kind of animal. Or more like some kind of baby, spitting up god knows what..."

"So what was wrong with it then?" Sally asked. "Did you find anything in your examination? Is it like maybe in H. G. Wells, that it's just not immune to our Earth germs yet, so maybe it's got a cold or something except that it's life-threatening to whatever it is..."

Dr. Ramson waved to her to be quiet. "It doesn't work that way," he said. "Rather it's more the opposite, that even if it had some kind of sickness, it won't affect us. Since it's not even human itself, it's not going to have any human diseases—especially not with the military making sure nobody even gets near it. Not anything we could catch."

Sally frowned. "Still, Doctor, I wish you'd call the hospital to have them come for these bags early, not wait till more than two weeks from now when they make their ordinary rounds."

"And take a chance on them asking questions?" Dr. Ramson said. "Or if we even took them out of town somewhere ourselves and buried them, having someone eventually spot a flash of orange after a rainstorm or washout or something? No—especially not with this stuff. Especially not with those secrecy forms we signed. At least, when the hospital picks them up normally, the last thing they'll do is open them up to look inside. And, as for the alien itself, in my opinion it wasn't even sick—more like just a case of fatigue. So even if alien 'germs' were catching..."

Dr. Ramson was not a good role model, but, rather, cut corners a bit too much sometimes. Especially when he had to deal with the unconventional, even if it was only the things they taught at the hospital in his annual board-required classes, he tended to hide what he wasn't used to under the rug.

Or in the hall closet.

This time what it was in the bright orange bags wasn't germ-spread, but was something akin to an alien cancer, something that spawned through its host's body's liquids. And yet it was not quite a cancer either, but something in its own right semi-intelligent.

Thus it discovered quickly enough the bags that had already been in the closet, and, sending its tendrils through submicroscopic pores in the bags' plastic, analyzed what festered within them, and found it was good. Blood and urine samples. Scrapings of human flesh. Slowly, joining its several separately-bagged parts together as tendrils touched tendrils, others questing up and out, some tasting the leather grips on golf clubs, others sampling an old, fur-trimmed jacket, others the wooden floor, it grew and waited.

And grew in its hunger.

It grew for two weeks and a few days more, by now filling the closet, when primitive sensors detected sounds outside:

"I guess you're glad, Sally, it's time to take these out."

"You know I'm not going to touch them, Doctor, so don't even ask me. I'd really rather not even be standing here while you handle them, except that I want to spray inside there as soon as it's empty."

"Yeah, you've told me often enough. Still, you've got to admit there was nothing to worry about, not even with this stuff..."

As often as not, Dr. Ramson was not a very good diagnostician either.

BACKGROUND FOR
THE COUNTRY DOCTOR

What real world conspiracy theory inspired you?

Flying saucers (aka Unidentified Flying Objects or UFOs) and
the Air Force study from 1948 to 1969, ultimately called Project
Blue Book, concluding that the vast majority of sightings
could be explained, but also downplaying the fraction that
remained. Partly because of a not always disguised attempt at
discrediting the idea that some might be artificial constructs
of extraterrestrial origin, some people considered Project Blue
Book to be a cover-up, suppressing the "truth" for fear of causing
panic in the midst of already existing Cold War tensions. One
famous example of this distrust, alluded to as well in the story,
involved wreckage found near Roswell, New Mexico, where the
government ultimately admitted that what they had claimed was
a crashed weather balloon was in fact the remains of an at-that-
time secret high altitude military project, but which was still
"too little, too late" for those who believe it was an actual alien
flying disk.

What other ramifications do you foresee if it were true?

In general, if there were/are really alien beings observing the
Earth the ramifications could be quite great. Think of what
happened, say, to Pacific Islanders—or to our own Native
Americans—when European explorers discovered them. In the
case of the story, though, the effect may be more immediate as
what amounts to a semi-intelligent alien disease is about to be
unleashed from the doctor's closet.

What media was crucial to your research?

I'm old enough to remember the time when UFOs were still in
the public eye (Project Blue Book, for instance, wasn't shut down

until 1969). For brushing up, however, Wikipedia is helpful for such subjects as Unidentified Flying Object, Extraterrestrial Hypothesis (ETH), Project Blue Book, Roswell UFO Incident, and Area 51. I might add, re. details about handling and reporting biological waste, etc., that I have worked in a medical (optometry) clinic.

NIGHTMARE AGENT

Scott Harper

Victor Varney lounged deeply back into the plush brown leather sofa, admiring the spacious room. It was, appropriately enough, a presidential suite, nestled on the 60th floor of a ridiculously expensive hotel, and afforded ample area in which to move. His pale skin soaked in the moonlight streaming through the panes of the balcony window. Varney savored the uniqueness of his bloodline, which granted the ability to draw strength from the lunar beams. Yet there was an unnatural agitation festering in the air, creeping along his skin and portending of dire events to come.

It will be here soon.

The disturbance mirrored the discord that had been sowed recently in the country he both served and revered. A bombastic, orange-skinned outsider has ascended unexpectedly to the presidency, causing large segments of the population to resist and, in some cases, revolt. Protests and riots became the order of the day, and shootings of congressmen soon followed. The country seethed on the border of outright bedlam, making it ripe for plunder by the Agents of Chaos.

The shouts of men and the screams of his lover roused him from daylight slumber. He tossed aside the coffin lid, still blood drunk from hunting the previous night, only to be blinded by the light of numerous torches. Marcilla was torn from her resting place and born to the floor of the crypt, two villagers holding down each of her limbs as they draped her in ropes of pungent garlic. A bulky friar stood over her, shouting orders and raising high a gold crucifix.

Averting his eyes from the holy symbol, the vampire stumbled from the coffin and headed toward her. She was screaming, her lips bloody as the men pummeled her with fists and clubs, calling his name now as she had so many years before, when he had been just a mortal man.

Villagers, eyes glazed and whipped into a frenzy by the churchmen, attacked. He grabbed one man by the neck, broke him, and flung him into two others, knocking them senseless. Another buried a sword deep into his sternum, but the blade was common metal and caused no injury. He tore out the man's throat with long teeth, gulping the hot blood, invigorating and stimulating a berserker fury. Yet for each man that fell, three more rose to take his place. The vampire could sense magic in the air, sorcery being used to inflame these men. Such magics were within the power of segments of the church to command.

Then through the haze of bloodlust and battle two more villagers approached Marcilla. The first shoved a large plank of sharpened wood through her torso, pinning her to the floor, while the other cut off her head with a silvered axe.

The strength left his body and more attackers descended as the friar ordered another villager to set her writhing remains on fire.

Varney waited, elevated senses on high alert. The most recent attacks on congressmen had been particularly brutal, churning even his iron stomach. Instead of employing semi-psychotic, determined radicals with rifles (who often missed their intended targets and instead ended up slaying civilians), the Agents of Chaos had elected to hire some type of animal mercenary. Varney had inspected the corpses. The bodies looked like they had been put through a shredder. The manner in which the corpses had been slashed, and, in some cases, eaten, indicated that an unknown breed of lycanthrope was responsible.

Varney was not surprised when, presently, the wolf man Leon crashed through the window in a shower of metal and glass and writhing muscle.

Leon surveyed the room, sniffing the air and probing with his enhanced senses, then settled his yellow eyes on Varney. A look of disappointment settled on the creature's face.

"No POTUS?" he asked.

Varney curled bloodless lips in a mirthless smirk. "Come now, old friend, you know the game. Our intel is onto you and your employers. We're even a step or two ahead of you, planting false information through our informants. We're actually quite good at it—years of practice. The leader of the free world is situated somewhere nice and safe, free to tweet to his heart's content. You, on the other hand, have stepped into the proverbial hornet's nest."

"So I'm left with only a dead man instead? I'd recognize your graveyard scent anywhere, Varney."

Varney chuckled. "And I yours, Leon. That repugnant yet charming combination of sweat, piss, forest pine and wolfsbane is impossible to forget."

The creature laughed, his voice guttural, moonlight reflecting off his animal eyes. "Still towing the party line, I see. Nothing ever changes with you, Varney," the wolf man said through a mouth filled with sharp teeth. Leon had elected to remain in the bipedal man-wolf form tonight, an equal mix of both species, standing nearly seven feet in height. There was enough of the man left inside the beast for his words to remain comprehensible.

"Well now, old sport, that pretty much sums up my curse, doesn't it?" Varney's eyes glowed with the same animal intensity as those of the wolf man.

He awoke, red eyes snapping open, as his upper lip was pulled back from his teeth. An older man in a finely tailored dark suit and bow tie loomed over, his craggy features set in a look of determination that furrowed his forehead.

"Your teeth are more like a wolf's than a man's. I presume the stories are true, then," the man declared, the stench of whisky strong on his breath.

The vampire lay on the wet floor of a dark cell, lit by a small gas lamp on the wall. Thick iron chains bound his wrists and ankles. A group of Union soldiers encircled, joined by a contingent of men in white hoods. The white hoods were festooned in ropes of pungent garlic, and carried wooden stakes and axes, silver light reflecting from the blades.

The man released his hold and settled into a nearby wooden chair. Though not physically intimidating, he possessed an air of uncompromising authority. His face gleamed in sweat as his voice echoed in the room, commanding attention.

"Mr. James Brown, if that is really your true name, do you know who I am?" the man asked.

The vampire repressed a laugh at the mention of the current alias. It bore no relation to the name he'd been born with into a modest noble family over two centuries ago in a rural town in Portugal. And when, some thirty years later, the dark kiss of a countess brought him beyond the realm of death, he had taken on yet another identity.

The stench of the Marcilla's burning body was still fresh in mind when he had fled Europe and escaped its vampire pogroms. Assuming the identity of "James Brown" in Boston, he scraped together a "living" as a whaling boat deckhand. Whaling was harsh work, a far cry from the comfort and privilege bestowed by the countess; yet it allowed him to surreptitiously sate the red thirst without attacking humans. The folklore of the Undead was known even in this new world, populated as it was by refugees from Europe, and so an outbreak of bloodless corpses would no doubt draw the priests with their stakes and silver. He had been discreet, and seemed to have averted the disaster that claimed so many other Undead. Or so he had thought.

For a time he moved unnoticed amongst the crew. He regretted the savagery doled out on the magnificent leviathans that were butchered daily; yet the hidden beast, the red thirst that lurked just beneath the surface of cognizance, reveled in the cruelty and bloodshed. The weather, often stormy and overcast, afforded the opportunity to function in the daylight hours.

During the last voyage a titanic squall had broken the masts and sent most of the crew to a watery grave. Adrift with two remaining mortals in open water and unrelenting sunlight, with the days turning into weeks, he used the men for sustenance. Once they were gone, he languished in the ship's hold, biting into the corpses, attempting to draw out any remaining fluid, even going so far as to crack open the bones and suck the marrow within. He became jaundiced and emaciated, eyes little more than hollow black sockets in a skull-like face, fangs jutting over the bottom lip.

It was in this condition that he was found when the ship ran ashore near the Canadian border in late 1867. Shouts roused him from stupor. Union soldiers pulled him from the floor, forcing his claws from the corpses, surrounding. Blows from fists and rifle butts registered but caused no actual pain. One soldier shoved a sabre through his chest as others grappled with him. He thrashed about, inhuman strength sending the men flying like children's toys, their bodies crashing into the walls. Then the men regrouped and fired their rifles. The bullets pierced neck, skull and torso. Depleted and desiccated, he collapsed to the floor.

"Mr. Brown, I'm waiting," the man prompted.

Returning attention to the present dire circumstances, the vampire feigned ignorance.

"My name is Andrew Johnson. I'm the president of this country. It's been brought to my attention that you have committed some blasphemous acts for which you should be strung up and duly hung. And yet my counsel, my men, have explained to me that you are quite a unique individual, that in fact hanging you would actually serve no purpose, because we know that won't kill you, will it, Mr. Brown?"

The vampire looked on without emotion but was curious what the man knew.

"Apparently bullets cause you little damage as well. You were shot numerous times when you were taken into custody, yet I see no wounds now, only holes and dried blood. I've learned that your kind possess certain...skills...talents which might be useful to a young country like ours, a nation just beginning to build itself amidst a world of enemies. You would conduct...operations...in the name of this country and its leaders. During these operations, you would have free reign to satisfy your...needs. And I would be willing to...overlook...the two corpses you were found with on that whaling ship. Do you grasp the enormity of what I'm offering you, Mr. Brown?"

Johnson continued. "My sources have told me about the purge being conducted in Europe. I'm giving you a chance, an opportunity one of your kind has never been given before. To exist without fear, to find refuge in the storm. Knowledge that, as long you work for us, you will be protected from the Church and its hunters, that your daylight domain will remain secure, and that your financial assets will be sheltered. Do we have an understanding, Mr. Brown?"

He nodded in agreement.

"Good, then we are understood," Johnson replied. "And, of course, you realize that, should you ever betray me or the country, the deal will automatically be rescinded. You will be put to the final death," Johnson said as he gestured toward the white hoods. The vampire now saw that some of them carried crossbows with wooden shafts and silver heads.

Johnson continued. "But in your current malnourished state, you're not much use to us."

The president motioned to one of the attending soldiers. "Corporal Clay, if you would be so kind."

A grizzle bearded soldier came forward, drawing a weathered Bowie knife from his waistband. He positioned his hand over a tin cup on a nearby wooden table and sliced into the palm, drawing blood. Clay turned his palm over and let his blood drip into the cup, repeatedly pumping his hand into a fist to spur the blood flow. When he was finished he presented the cup to the vampire, who gripped it in clawed hands. Inhaling the heady smell of the liquid ambrosia, he downed the contents. The blood drove out the bitter cold that was saturating his lifeless veins. He crushed the cup in a display of renewed strength, eyes blazing in the darkness of the room.

He became an black mist, slipping from the chains, before rematerializing and offering a grimy claw and a toothy smile to the stunned president.

"Absolutely."

"Sealed in blood," replied the president, shocked by the coldness of the fingers that encircled his own in a grip of steel. He scrunched his face in an attempted grin as they shook hands.

And thus the world's first government vampire was hired.

The revenant's initial inclination had been to double cross this pompous man. He had little regard for European royalty, and had even less respect for this man of common blood who had not inherited, but rather, been elected to his office. After performing a few errands as instructed, he would disappear into the mists when no one was watching. These simple men had severely underestimated the true extent of his powers. Yet he soon realized there was no other home to flee to. And, as time wore on and the missions accumulated, he began to identify with this bastard country and its peoples and struggles. The initial assignments took a number of varied turns, from protecting newly freed slaves in the South from attacks by their former warlock owners to thwarting an invasion of Massachusetts by fish men. Many nights were spent in Pittsburgh graveyards, granting second deaths to hordes of the dead being raised by a cabal of necromancers.

Over time, the varied enemies of America formed a coalition, led by a splinter group from the church known as the Agents of Chaos. He found a purpose that had been missing before, a drive beyond the simple physical need for fresh blood that, up until this point, had consumed the entirety of existence. And when Johnson's successor, a gruff soldier statesman with a penchant for directness, asked him to continue service, the vampire had consented. And he continued to consent to serve twenty-seven successive presidents after that.

Varney smiled and stood, adjusting the front of an outdated pinstripe suit out of habit. "I see you've changed since you left the agency, Leon. Selling your services to the highest bidder, I assume? And the anarchists and currency manipulators of the world, those men in league with Chaos, have plenty of money to pay for your...unique...talents?"

The beast snorted, showing his black gums and yellow teeth. "Hell, what can I say? Some of these guys think carbon emissions and micro-aggressions are the biggest evils the world has ever seen. Who am I, a dumb and simple werewolf, to tell them otherwise?"

"You know better, Leon." Varney's face became grim. "You've seen first-hand the real evils of the world—children in Africa kidnapped and forced into slavery...human trafficking in Mexico. People in North Korea starved while their leaders live in luxury and build weapons that can destroy the planet over and over. Non-violent worshipers rounded up and executed for practicing their minority religion in the Middle East. You had a chance to change that, to redeem yourself after a lifetime of evil. You came to the agency a broken man, having just slaughtered a family of innocents in Yugoslavia, seeking some form of redemption. The Agency channeled your rage, gave you a focus and a purpose. Together, we made a difference. Now that's all gone."

Leon shook his head in disapproval. "I got tired of all that nonsense, Victor. In the end, nothing really changes. We take out one bad guy, two more spring up to take his place. This country we fought for is more divided than ever. It's rotting from within. All this talk of banning immigrants? Last I checked the people in this country are pretty damned good at dividing themselves up and finding reasons to hate and kill each other without outside help. Hah! And what do I really care, one way or another? Unless someone shoots me with a silver bullet or skewers me with a silver sword, I will live on, cursed, till the end of time. Hell, Victor, I wonder if we both could live through the next nuclear holocaust." His fur bristled and the muscles on his gargantuan frame tensed.

Varney sensed the resolution in the wolf man's voice. "It doesn't have to end this way," he offered in a last attempt at civility, a quality of diminishing importance in this new world. Still, he girded for battle, sclera bleeding crimson, ears lengthening, claws sprouting from spiderlike fingers.

"Oh, it was always gonna end this way, Victor" Leon continued. "Mission or no mission, hired assassin or government monster, I've always wanted to be the one to tear that smug look off your aristocrat face!"

Leon executed a mammoth leap across the room. Varney met his charge, grabbing the beast's furred arms at the wrists. For a moment the two engaged in a titanic battle of supernatural strength. Leon was the larger of the two, his frame bulging with thick slabs of muscle, and sought to press that advantage, struggling to force Varney to the ground. Varney countered with a strength greater than that of twenty men, driving the wolf man back. Frustrated, a furious Leon snarled and lunged forward, attempting to bite Varney's neck. The vampire agent countered with a head butt, breaking teeth and sending the wolf man reeling back into a dresser drawer.

The creature recovered almost instantly. In an awesome display of power, Leon hefted the large drawer over his head with ease, his claws digging into the wood. He slung it at Varney, who dodged the improvised missile with unnatural speed and agility.

Closing the distance, he delivered a roundhouse punch to the wolf man's jaw. The blow forced Leon to his knees. Varney attempted to land a second blow, only to reel back, throat sliced open from a back swipe of Leon's claws.

Viscous blood seeped from the massive wound. Such an injury would have killed a human. Varney, however, was only inconvenienced and willed the wound to close.

Leon sought to press his advantage. He unleashed a series of claw strikes, snarling and growling. The vampire agent ducked and weaved, using preternatural reflexes to avoid the majority of the attacks. One blow landed, rocking Varney's head back and tearing off a large patch of skin. He staggered back into a wall. The wolf man, poised on what he believed was the edge of victory, drew back his left claw and readied the final blow.

The vampire slipped into the room on the Jersey Shore, the stench of death lingering in the stale air. The president, a man named Garfield, lay insensate on a bed, slowing dying from an infected gunshot wound. The vampire could smell pus and blood and other liquids oozing from the wound. The mortal doctors, in their noble yet short-sighted attempts to save the man, had actually inflicted worse injury upon him, even puncturing his liver.

The president slowly drew breath in and out over chapped lips. The vampire noted another mortal in the room, a doctor who, tasked with monitoring the dying leader, had conveniently fallen asleep.

Once, such a sight of mortal suffering would not have caused distress. However, over the years of service to this new country, he had developed an appreciation for just how fragile the democratic republic was, and what the death of its leader might entail. He regretted his failure to prevent the shooting some months earlier.

He'd tracked the eventual assassin, a lunatic named Charles Guiteau, to a boarding house in Washington, near the Baltimore and Potomac Railroad Station. Guiteau had made no secret of his enmity for the newly elected president, going so far as to send a letter to General Sherman informing the Commanding General of the Army of his intentions to assassinate Garfield. The vampire had intended to discreetly dispose of Guiteau in his room and then move on. He was not prepared for the maelstrom that waited, for it was not Guiteau waiting inside, but rather a demon from Hell itself.

He would later learn that the Agents of Chaos had chosen Guiteau as their instrument and guided his path toward the president. To that end they had summoned a demon from some God-forsaken side pool dimension, making whatever blood sacrifices were necessary to appease the dark forces and bridge the barrier between worlds. The vampire was caught off-guard when the beast, a gargantuan, multi-eyed conglomeration of bat and bear and pig and wolf, attacked.

After a prolonged battle, during which large sections of the house were destroyed, he had triumphed, managing to tear both bile-pumping green hearts from the demon's chest. The victory had come at great cost, the beast's teeth and claws inflicting numerous wounds that healed slowly. In addition, the demon's blood had contaminated the wounds, acting like poison. The vampire had been crawling toward the front door of the house when the shots that fell the president boomed.

His sense of regret was almost palpable. He had the power to save this fallen mortal, to bring him across the barrier of death.

His teeth lengthened in anticipation. He took one step toward Garfield.

Yet, the memory of his own turning informed that the president that emerged would be a changed being, no longer human, and far removed from the essential mortal capacities for compassion and empathy. And so he reluctantly chose to turn away and leave as his president died.

There will, no doubt, be others that follow.

Leon struck, a grin on his face. Instead of cold flesh, however, his claw passed through an insubstantial mist and embedded itself in the wall. The wolf man was in a shocked state of confusion when strong hands grabbed and lifted him, tossing him with ease back across the room. He struck the opposite wall like a handball and bounced off, coming to rest heavily on his back. His hands were pinned to the floor as Varney climbed like a spider on top of him.

"End of the road, chum."

Leon coughed up blood, his rib cage broken, clearly defeated. "How can you do it, Varney? How can you look at yourself? You work for an arrogant, illiterate, petulant, orange-skinned child. He's a fraud, a charlatan, a mistake. Never in my lifetime has there been a man so unworthy of the office."

Varney smiled. "Well now, old sport, that's never really been the issue, has it? This country, this political entity, must...will go on, no matter who is in charge. And these people, even as vicious and divided as they are, as petty as they can be...they deserve to be protected from the monsters of the world. The true monsters. Creatures like you. Creatures like me. I know what I am, deep inside, Leon. Fiend. Vampire. Blood Sucker. Night Walker. And one day perhaps I'll lose control. One day perhaps someone will be forced to drive an ash stake through my heart and cut off my head and burn the remains and scatter them on the wind. But that day is not today."

Leon smiled, his teeth chipped and bloody. His voice was weak when he spoke. "You can't kill me, Victor. There's no silver in this room. I can sense it. I've still got all the time in the world."

"You've got a lot to learn, my friend. Humans need silver to hurt you. I'm not human. Unfortunately for you, time is a luxury you no longer possess."

The vampire agent bit deep into the wolf man's neck. Leon's eyes rolled back in his head as he was exsanguinated. When his heart beat no more, he returned to his human form. Varney whispered into the corpse's ear.

"Administrations, like countries, come and go. But Victor Varney is eternal."

The vampire rose from the kill, brimming with energy from the inhuman blood. Arms raised high and wide, he stretched and embraced the moonlight, encarmined lips peeling back from fangs.

Sublime!

A part of him regretted the kill, the tiny shred of being that remained of the soul. But the Undead had no souls, not really. They lost that tie to humanity when they crossed over. And perhaps that lost soul was the motivation that that fueled the urge to seek some form of redemption, even after all these years. The reason he still stuck to a foolish bargain made centuries ago with a man long dead and forgotten. Why he continued to fight for the integrity of a country, of a cause, that many nowadays laughed at and mocked. Maybe, someday, he might reclaim his own soul.

The notion lent hope, an essential component of existence, even for a dead man. His arms lengthened into wings of dark membrane and he took flight.

BACKGROUND FOR
NIGHTMARE AGENT

***What historical period did you choose and what attracted
you to it?***
The bulk of my story is set in the present and focuses on the
current political turbulence in the United States. Owing to the
vampiric nature of my protagonist, the story also features a
number of flashbacks that detail the evolution of his character
over centuries.

***What did you change and what do you see the fallout from
it to be?***
I added a supernatural element to world history — essentially
the same major historical events occurred in my alternative
timeline/multiverse, but were manipulated by monsters and
other weird entities. The world I created is a darker, uglier
version of our current version, but still offers the possibility of
redemption.

What texts were crucial to your research?
The history of "vampire" James Brown and his pardon by
President Andrew Johnson in 1867 was first referenced in a story
in *The Brooklyn Daily Eagle* dated November 4, 1892. The incident
would later be referenced by American author Charles Fort in his
1933 book, *Wild Talents*. Brown's story is also included in Robert
Damon Schneck's collection of odd but true tales, *The President's
Vampire*.

For different takes on a vampire working as a government agent,
I highly recommend Gordon Linzer's *The Spy Who Drank Blood*
as well as Christopher Farnsworth's *Blood Oath*.

What is a good introduction to this period?

I would suggest *Resistance (At All Costs)* by Kimberley Strassel, a well-researched work on recent American political history.

THE WALRUS
Vonnie Winslow Crist

Gilroy Puddleton was witness to the accident that changed rock and roll history—only most people didn't know history had been changed. He'd been just off the roadway changing a flat tire in the early hours of the morning when a speeding auto crashed into a parked van about ten meters to his left. For a few seconds (he really couldn't be sure of the exact number of seconds, since he'd been in shock at seeing such a thing), Gilroy had stood still as a tombstone with his heart racing and his mouth gaping. Then his senses returned, and he dropped the tire iron and ran over to the smashed automobile.

Confident in skills learned at a recent first aide class and eager to offer assistance, Gilroy pushed up his sleeves and leaned inside the smashed vehicle. The predawn light revealed a headless corpse and a second mangled body pinned inside. After emptying the contents of his stomach, Gilroy managed to get back to his parents' sedan and sit in the front seat.

He thought of running to the nearest house and asking to use the telephone, but it was unnecessary. A woman wearing nightclothes with curlers still in her hair hurried toward the accident screaming, "I've phoned for help. Is there anything we can do?"

"No," he answered. "They're dead."

"Oh, my," the woman replied. Without another word, she walked back to her home.

Law enforcement personnel arrived at the scene quickly, and it became evident to Gilroy that someone of importance had died. In the commotion that followed their arrival, he was sure he heard the words, "It's one of the Beatles," and "It's Paul," and "Such a shame."

The area was rapidly corded off, traffic was diverted, and a squad of serious-looking men dressed in drab clothing arrived. The men-in-grey quickly dispersed the crowd and set up a barricade far from the accident scene. As for Gilroy, they insisted he stay in his car and wait to talk to the police. But it wasn't the police who came to speak with him.

A tall, official-looking man wearing glasses and carrying a clipboard approached Gilroy. "Name? Address? Occupation?" he asked.

"Gilroy Puddleton, accountant. I live with my parents at…" He gave the official his parents' address, then asked, "Can you tell me if that was Paul from the Beatles?"

The man lowered his clipboard. "Stay here," he ordered.

Two other men returned with the tall man. "We understand you were witness to the accident," began the shortest of the men who wore a fedora, "but we need to keep this particular event from the news."

"I see," said Gilroy. Well, he thought, that confirms the headless man was one of the Beatles. It was immediately clear to him that such a tragedy would alter the future of the singing group. It might even be a career-breaker, since according to his neighbors, Paul was the "cute one" they all loved.

"We're prepared to make you a sizable offer to keep silent."

"You're bribing me?"

Any hint of a smile vanished from the faces of the three men.

"Think of it as a gift we're giving to you in order to spare the victim's family, the fans, the record company, the touring company, the band, and so many others from the sorrow and horror of this ill-timed accident," said the man in the fedora. Taking Gilroy's lack of response as a sign of resistance, the man continued, "We want things to continue forward for the group as if this never happened, and we're willing to do what is necessary to keep this death a secret."

Suddenly, Gilroy realized he could either shut up or end up buried in an unmarked spot in a lonely field somewhere in Scotland.

"How much?" he asked.

The trio smiled while Mr. Fedora explained the amount and method of payment. As Gilroy nodded his head, he glanced at the policemen who were talking with other members of the men-in-grey squad. He knew no one here today would go to the papers. Everyone would benefit financially, or find themselves beneath the sod.

Thus, Gilroy Puddleton, accountant, ended up with a tidy sum in his bank account. But the money brought him little happiness. Over the next two years, while the Fab Four made music history, both of his parents died and the girl he had taken a fancy to eloped with a bloke who was the night shift bartender at the Kirk Street Pub.

As for Gilroy, he continued to work for the same company, adopted a stray tabby and named her Mrs. Whiskers, and spent his spare time puttering around the garden and collecting information on the conspiracy surrounding Paul McCartney's 1966 death. A death Gilroy knew in fact had occurred, though he dared not tell a soul the truth about what happened.

He became fixated on the new and old Beatles. When a certain William Campbell, winner of a Paul McCartney lookalike competition and an orphan from Edinburgh, vanished immediately after the accident, Gilroy knew he'd been brought in as a replacement. Supposedly able to sing like the original and a songwriter himself, Gilroy imagined William Campbell was a dream come true for those trying to keep Paul alive. They just needed to teach the right hander to play guitar with his left hand.

Gilroy was certain it was no coincidence the Beatles stopped touring in fall 1966 right after the auto wreck. He knew plastic surgeons needed time to make the replacement resemble the original Paul as closely as possible. A replacement, he noted in his files, who chose to grow a mustache to hide the fact that his lips were different from the original Paul's lips.

More troubling than the difference in lip spacing, was the crooked tooth. Comparing photographs from early 1966 with later pictures, Gilroy saw a surgeon had carefully made one of the replacement's front teeth crooked. But the doctor couldn't reshape the new Paul's palette without extensive braces and other mouth apparatus which would have had to been on the replacement's teeth for a year and probably would have altered the new Paul's voice. But you had to look closely at the photos with a magnifying glass to even notice—and most people were satisfied to believe the current Beatles were the original Beatles and let sleeping dogs lie.

It was with some delight that Gilroy read an article in an Italian paper prepared by a forensic pathologist specializing in craniometry and odontology and a computer analysis specialist. The duo had entered into the "Paul is Dead" conspiracy mirk with the goal of disproving the conspiracy, but instead the results of their investigation seemed to prove that the original Paul had been killed in an auto accident.

Using good photos from private collections from both before and after the rumored accident, the pair had resized the pictures. Using the distance between the pupils of the eyes on the pre-accident Paul as the scaling factor, they'd done a proper comparison. They said though skin, hair, and other surface features might change, the shape of the skull didn't alter. When a post-accident photograph was laid on top of a pre-accident picture of Paul, they should match. But the skulls didn't match. Nor did the frontal curvature of the jawline. The jawline from ear to ear of the new Paul didn't line up with the jawline of the old Paul.

The Italian team also pointed out that the shape of the ear was unique—so unique that in Germany, it was used for identification much like a fingerprint or DNA evidence. They placed a picture of the old Paul's and new Paul's right ear side-by-side. Even to an amateur sleuth, it was clearly not the same ear.

Still, no one from the British government investigated the conspiracy. Gilroy wondered if they had known a young woman was also killed in that wreck, too, would it have made a difference? Didn't her family have a right to know their daughter was dead? A right to bury her in a family kirkyard?

Thoughts of the dead girl—he'd read her name was Rita in a conspiracy newsletter—gnawed at him. His parents would have wanted to know what had happened if Gilroy had been killed in a crash. He decided he should try to find and contact Rita's parents. He would do so anonymously. The men-in-grey would never know. And so, Gilroy Puddleton began a course of action.

While he searched for the identity of Rita (hopefully, that was her real name), Gilroy came across an article from Germany about a woman who was supposed to be Paul's daughter from before the accident. His name had even been listed on her birth certificate. The new Paul had been paying thousands of dollars to support her, but then, she'd demanded a DNA test. The new Paul had taken the test and, of course, he wasn't her father. He'd even signed his name on the paperwork—with a right-handed signature. The woman had accused the man who took the DNA test of being an impostor—but again, hush money appeared to have settled the dispute.

Finally, Gilroy reached the end of his rope. As he leafed through the notebooks of evidence he'd gathered, he decided to share his findings and witness testimony with a reporter. He'd carefully documented all of the evidence in the 1967 *Magical Mystery Tour* album, the cover photograph of the *Abbey Road* album where Paul was barefoot, and when John said Paul was the walrus in the lyrics of "Glass Onion" on his *White Album*. Gilroy believed John finally wanted to come clean, and was assassinated to keep him quiet. Perhaps, George's illness was induced by men-in-grey determined to keep a long-held secret. It appeared to him that Ringo was the only one smart enough to stay silent.

He wondered about the policemen at the scene of the crash, the medical personnel at the morgue, the surgeons who changed William Campbell into the new Paul, even the woman in her nightclothes—had everyone been paid off? Or had they been erased?

It was with shaking hand Gilroy called a reporter from a London paper. He left a message on the woman's answering machine telling her he had proof Paul had been killed in a 1966 auto accident after a row with his band mates sent him speeding away from the recording studio. He asked her to return his call and left his phone number and address.

While awaiting her phone call, Gilroy went to his bedroom closet, climbed onto a step ladder, reached into the back corner of the shelf above the rod where he hung his trousers, and grabbed a cardboard box. The original Mrs. Whiskers and her two replacements now dead, Thursday night the fourth Mrs. Whiskers mewed at Gilroy as he opened the box and removed a plastic bag containing a bloodstained shirt. This was the shirt Gilroy had worn those many mornings ago when he'd gone to the side of the smashed auto to see if he could help. Paul's blood was on the right sleeve.

DNA testing was more advanced nowadays. If the replacement Paul refused to be involved, he knew the authorities could request legal paperwork to get blood from one of the original Paul's relatives. Even a mild-mannered accountant's word would be believed if he had DNA evidence that the original Paul was killed in 1966. He wondered if there would be any legal consequences for the new Paul, Ringo, the police, the men-in-grey...

He set the shirt down when he heard a knock on his door. Perhaps the reporter had been coming this way and decided to just stop by. He didn't mind. He lived an ordinary life with few pressing responsibilities, so an unexpected visitor was a welcome diversion.

Gilroy opened the door expecting to see a semi-famous, thirty-something, bespectacled reporter standing on the porch. "What! Who are..."

Four men-in-grey pushed their way into his living room.

"Where is it?" asked the one with the gun.

Too frightened to argue, Gilroy pointed at the plastic bag resting on a coffee table in the center of the room.

"Couldn't let it go?" said an old man in a fedora.

"Wait, you're from..."

"True," replied Mr. Fedora before turning to one of his minions and ordering him to gather anything having to do with the Beatles.

Before he could protest, Gilroy found himself gagged and his hands secured behind his back with a plastic tie by the other two men-in-grey.

"Well, it's in the boot and off to the highlands for you, chap," said Mr. Fedora as the men who'd gagged and bound Gilroy tossed his bedspread over his head. "Tie him up good. We don't want any slip-ups," added the man. "Oh, and let the cat out—no sense in locking it in here to starve to death. A neighbor is likely to adopt a nice looking tabby."

At least he has a soft heart when it comes to animals, thought Gilroy as he was loaded into a large auto's boot. I'd hate to think of Mrs. Whiskers suffering in my absence.

Before the automobile pulled away as Gilroy Puddleton listened to the plaintive meows of Mrs. Whiskers, he suspected with his demise and the destruction of the bloody shirt, the cover up of Paul McCartney's death would be complete.

BACKGROUND FOR
THE WALRUS

What historical period did you choose and what attracted you to it?

I chose the 1960s. It was the decade I moved from childhood into my teens. I played 45s on my record player, danced in the garage, and embraced the rock-and-roll music coming to the USA from Great Britain.

What did you change and what do you see the fallout from it to be?

I changed to fact the rumor that Paul McCartney died in a November 9, 1966 auto accident, and was replaced by William Shears Campbell, a McCartney look-alike, so the Beatles could continue to perform.

When the Beatles arrived on the international music stage, they quickly became the most popular recording and performing band in the world. Between appearances, records, and merchandise sales, the Beatles generated an enormous amount of money. Paul McCartney, besides being John Lennon's writing partner, was considered by fans to be the "cute" one. Had he disappeared from the group, it would've damaged their popularity and altered their future. The impact of the Beatles and their music on rock-and-roll and the culture of the 1960s would've been lessened. So the false "Paul McCartney" (Billy Shears) kept the Beatles whole, and wrote *Let it Be, Hey Jude, Lady Madonna, St. Pepper's Lonely Heart Club's Band*, and many other songs.

What texts were crucial to your research?
operationreachthelost.com/ringo-starr-claims-real-paul-mccartney-died-1966-replaced-look-alike/

nationalpost.com/news/world/i-buried-paul-your-guide-to-the-convoluted-conspiracy-that-paul-mccartney-died-in-1966

plasticmacca.blogspot.com/2010/01/forensic-science-proves-paul-was.html

rollingstone.com/music/music-news/paul-mccartney-is-dead-musics-most-wtf-conspiracy-theories-explained-120340/

What is a good introduction to this period?
Any book on the early Beatles or the 1960s would work.
A couple that come to mind: *The Beatles: The Biography* by Bob Spitz and *The 1960s: American Popular Culture Through History* by Edward J. Rielly.

MOTIVATED MILITIA

A *Throne of Hearts* short story
Gil Hough

As Jesse pulled his old SUV into the small parking lot of the County offices, he was disappointed with the building's style. He had hoped for something with a little more character, but the building looked like a block of concrete designed to be ugly.

"What are we going to do with Scooby?" asked Belinda.

"Ahh, the perennial question, now that our little malformed puppy has grown into a huge warped monstrosity," answered Jesse.

A slobbering massive canine head covered in loose folds of skin immediately emerged between the two front seats and showed him lots of pointed white teeth.

"Just kidding, my furry friend," Jesse hurriedly added. He said in a wistful tone, "You know, when I was a kid, my dog did not know when I was insulting him. I miss those days."

Belinda pointedly ignored Jesse's conversation with himself and asked Scooby, "If we let you out of the car, you promise not to wander off?" When the Dorg nodded and bumped his head on the passenger door, Belinda got out and opened it up. The great beast jumped down and then covered a small tree in pee.

"He would probably scare people less if he was tied up," said Jesse in a carefully neutral voice.

"Very true. Why don't you go put the rope on him? I'll watch the show," she responded with a smile. The whiteness of her teeth was highlighted by her skin's very dark color .

She had a breathtaking smile, he thought, but he still felt awkward being so much taller than her. When he had first met her less than a year ago, he had been only an inch taller than the five-foot ten young woman. Now he was at least four inches taller.

As the two started walking towards the glass doors that led inside, he started looking for directions, but other than a sign that said, "Cronin Township Offices," there was nothing to see. He whispered, "What is the difference between a town and a township?"

"No idea," she whispered back.

A woman sat behind a long counter as they entered; no one else was in the building's foyer, and they stood quietly as she finished up on the phone which seemed to be someone complaining about an electric bill.

"Yes, can I help you?" asked the woman who Jesse thought looked older than she probably was.

"We have an appointment with the Township Manager, a Mr. Fisher," explained Belinda.

"If you are another Black Lives Matter protester..." responded the woman, her voice rising as she spoke.

"What? Why would I be a BLM protestor just because I am black?" asked Belinda.

Jesse cut in, "Jesse Vanderson and Belinda Abernathy. We are expected by Mr. Fisher. Can you see if he is available?"

She gave them a long look, then picked up the phone and hit a button and said quietly, "Phil, I got a couple out here, a black girl and a big ugly bruiser, they said you were expecting them?"

They were soon in the office of the Township Manager, a not very impressive looking office with loose papers everywhere and the general look of someone with either a lot of work or a very odd filing system. The office did boast a nice pair of comfortable guest chairs.

"Just call me Phil," Mr. Fisher said as he sat down behind his old wooden desk. He appeared to be in his mid-forties with short dirty blond hair. He was trim, with the build of someone who kept in shape by running.

"I appreciate you two driving to the middle of nowhere Michigan from Tennessee. How was the trip?"

Belinda said, "The last few hours were beautiful, though I assume it must get cold up here this far north and close to Lake Michigan. But, unless you found more money in your budget, we are on the clock, and your retainer will not go far. So, we would like to get right to work."

"Sure, sure...I appreciate that. This might sound weird; God knows the Feds think I am nuts, as does the Special Unit of the Michigan Bureau of Investigations."

Jesse just smiled—he knew how desperate the official had to be to hire them. They didn't even have a website; someone must have given them a recommendation.

"So, you have been very vague about your problem. You said we had to come up here to understand it? But your town doesn't seem under attack by a supernatural creature," asked Belinda.

"That's just it, people here are the salt of the earth. They have known each other for generations, and we take care of each other. We have no problems, at least nothing serious," he stated before asking, "Have you been watching what has been happening in Lansing?"

At their blank look, he added helpfully, "Michigan's capital. It has been all over the news—heavily armed militia men going up to the capitol steps and saying all this crazy stuff. Conspiracy nonsense, and other crap. It takes five seconds to fact check to know it is all stupid, but most of the crazies are all coming from this township—good, honest people that have suddenly gone off their rocker!"

"And you think it is some supernatural influence?" guessed Jesse.

"Has to be!" agreed Phil. "It is the only thing that makes sense."

Belinda nodded, but pointed out in her usual practical way, "It is probably just social media, pushed no doubt by nefarious groups trying to set Americans against each other. What makes you think there is something supernatural going on?"

"Look, we have more militia than any state per capita. We are an independent-minded folk, but we aren't stupid." The man was getting worked up, and Jesse could see him take a few deep breaths before saying, "Look, I'm paying you. Please look around. You two are supposed to be good at finding trouble."

Jesse had to admit that the last part was hard to argue with, and while the money was modest, it was money, and they were struggling to pay the bills. "Any thoughts on where to look?"

"Sure, the Mountain Sparrows is a militia camp just five miles to the east of here. I would suggest you go in the morning. You do not want to be out there at night. It's been there for decades, but it seems to be the center of whatever is happening."

Belinda nodded and said, "That sounds like a solid lead, we will see what we can do," and reached out a hand to Phil. Jesse followed her lead and shook his hand. Soon enough, they were all climbing back in the car.

To their relief, a mob had not gathered around Scooby. He gathered attention. Luckily, he was also exceptionally good at charming people, so they were alarmed at first, but then Belinda and Jesse had to pry people off the Dorg.

Before climbing in the car, Jesse licked his finger, stuck it up into the air, and then looked up at the treetops. Belinda nodded at seeing his action.

"So, I assume we will not follow Phil's recommendation for waiting till morning? Is it time to actually make Scooby earn his keep?" she asked.

Jesse nodded, "He's probably going to run out into the woods either way. If he is part of an operation, he won't go howling and barking at every squirrel he sees. Plus, we have advantages in the dark that the militia men won't."

"Other than knowing their home terrain," agreed Belinda.

"I know some of these types from back in the hills of North Carolina. It would not surprise me to find booby traps and all sorts of crazy stuff around the perimeter of their camp," warned Jesse.

Belinda's eyebrows went up at that. She was a city girl, but she could handle herself in the woods if needed. Two hours later found them in the woods, a little over a mile east of where the Mountain Sparrows camp was supposed to be. It was getting dark fast, but with the wind coming from the West, they trusted Scooby's abilities to find the camp.

"I really don't enjoy sneaking into a camp of heavily armed men with our guns in the car," Jesse whispered for the third time to Belinda.

"We might feel better, but as far as we know, these are just people, not vampires, not Grigori or another kind of supernatural creatures. If they see a few armed people sneaking into camp, bullets will start flying, people will die."

"I know intellectually that having a gun makes you less safe," agreed Jesse. " But it sure would make me feel better with my old 10 mm in my hand."

"In case you forgot," reminded Belinda, "We at least try to be the good guys. That means we are willing to take risks so that innocents don't die."

Jesse just nodded and let it drop. He knew it was the right thing to do. He was just letting off steam by complaining.

As the sun fell behind the horizon, the forest fell into deep darkness. It should have been a little scary, but as the last vestiges of the light disappeared, energy filled the two of them that they had both shared since they had first met as part of a Slice and Dice crew helping clean out a nest of vampires—a nest that had proven to have far more going on than anyone had known. While the night got dark, all their senses came alive: sound, smell, even the feel of the ground-oriented them in subtle ways.

"Go on, boy," whispered Belinda to Scooby, "Don't go all the way in, but get us to this Mountain Sparrow camp. Keep your eyes out for traps, but we'll keep up."

The Dorg gave a low, deep woof and bound into the woods; Jesse and Belinda bound behind. The two lost themselves in the challenge of running through a dark wood. It was beautiful, and for a while, they shared no words as they lost themselves in the simple task.

Their wild run through the woods came to a sudden end when Scooby came to a quick halt, and his tail went up, and he became utterly still.

The huge Dorg seemed to sniff at something and made an alarmed snort. Belinda and Jesse got down on their knees and tried to see what had the Dorg's attention.

Belinda pointed at something right by the canine's nose and said, "There is a thin taunt wire right in front of him."

"Tripwire?" asked Jesse. "These mothers are not messing around."

"Scooby, you stay out here, scouting the perimeter. Don't come unless we call you and keep your eye out for more of these traps," the Dorg just nodded and backed up and started circling around.

"It sounds like we are close," Jesse said, referencing the sound of men and women talking that he was sure she could also hear.

She nodded as she slowly stepped over the tripwire and said, "One step at a time from here, slow and easy."

Jesse nodded and did his best to shut down his tendency to say random things during times of danger. Finally, they came across an old rusted-out school bus, and both peeked around the corner at an odd combination of sheds, a large campfire, strings of lights, and what appeared to be dug in cover spots surrounded by sandbags.

They heard someone in the woods approaching from their right; without a word, they backed up deeper into the woods.

"Why don't we ask the guard what is going on?" whispered Belinda.

Jesse nodded with a smile, they went low, and he got behind a tree. Belinda, whose slim build did not need much space, simply sank down low around a bush. The man had a flashlight, but it seemed to be shining up around into the trees more than the path. Belinda was the first to move, leaping out at the man, her right hand around his mouth, and delivering a shocking, powerful blow into his gut from her left fist. The man folded.

Jesse had followed like a shadow, but there was no need for him to do anything other than help hold the man down. The guard proved to be even younger than Jesse, maybe nineteen, but he wore army fatigues, a bullet-proof vest, and an assault rifle, now pinned below him. He panted heavily, having lost his breath but did not look as shocked by the attack as you would expect.

"We have some questions for you," Belinda harshly said in low tones. "Answer honestly, and we won't hurt you."

"Yeah," growled Jesse, "Spartans or Wolverines? The green or the blue and gold? Your life depends on your answer."

Belinda made a familiar sighing sound at his irrelevant question, even as a slight smile crossed her lips. "Actually, we've heard there is something odd going on here at the camp. Tell us what it is, and we'll free you."

The young man looked back and forth at the two figures and seemed to squint, trying to get a good look at them. The flashlight was in the bushes, and he couldn't see his attackers in the dark. When Jesse gave him a little shake, he said, "Go Blue, and I do not understand what you are talking about."

"Crap," Belinda said, snatching her hands back from the prone man.

Then Jesse felt it and snatched his hands away. "Snake!" Dang, he realized they must have pushed the man on top of a snake and trapped it under him.

"Trespassers! Invaders!" screamed the young man.

"God dang it!" Jesse thought, as he made a fist and punched the man hard enough in the face to take him out of commission. Both he and Belinda jumped up, but flashlights were snapping on from every direction.

"That's impossible. They knew we were here," said Belinda. She was not whispering, as there was no point now.

Jesse thought about going for the assault rifle under the unconscious man, but the flashlights and the heavily armed men were closing in from every direction. If it had been vampires or the like, he would have done it no matter the odds, but when Belinda raised her arms up in surrender, he followed her lead by standing up and raising his hands up.

The men who came in were dressed like the young man at their feet, but it was not a proper uniform. The colors and designs varied wildly, and, while they were all heavily armed, like a soldier in the field, they sported every kind of imaginable gun.

As the men pushed them to the ground and tied their hands up with zip cords, Jesse thought the major difference to actual professional soldiers was their age and weight; most were in their forties or older and were forty or fifty pounds overweight, with one or two being twice that.

They were pulled back to their feet and led by gunpoint into camp. Strangely, no one asked them questions, and Jesse saw no signs of leadership.

They left the young man on the ground as if they were not concerned at all by his fate. Jesse warned the man on his right, who sported an impressively long beard, about the snake under the young man, but the only reply he got was, "Shut up and walk."

While there was no conversation among the men, there was some grumbling, mostly swear words followed by either "deep state" or "trying to take our freedom!".

They were quickly led into one of the larger buildings, which seemed to be an oversized two-car metal garage, but there were no signs of any cars or tools. Instead, there was an old radio set up on a long table to the side, a TV, and some chairs in a corner which seemed to have FOX News on, and two old refrigerators.

The main decorations seemed to be beer cans and beer bottles, which were everywhere.

The room had a half a dozen women waiting for the men to return; their clothes were similar but lacked the bullet-proof vests and assault weapons, but several sported pistols. Two overweight women with long dirty blond hair, who might have been sisters, wore a pair of neon pink pistols in holsters on their hips.

The weirdest thing to Jesse was that still, no one talked; people swore and made comments, but no one asked any questions or spoke to each other. More people filed in, both men and women, and most carried handheld drums of all kinds as they gathered in a circle.

Finally, no more people came in. Someone turned the TV off, and another person pushed him to move. The group in the center seemed to walk in a circle while the others all pulled back forming an outer circle. Someone behind him cut his hands free of the cord that had bound him. He rubbed his wrists in relief. The scruffy man with the long beard he had tried to talk to before pushed him and said, "Dance."

"What?" Jesse said in confusion.

"Dance!" commanded a handful of people who were closest to them, the voice in a strange harmony. Simultaneously, people in the outer circle started beating the drums; it started off randomly, but a strange beat that he was not familiar with became clear. Now, everyone spoke as one to both him and Belinda, "DANCE!"

People started pushing and pulling him, and he realized that there were four couples in the inner circle with him and Belinda, and they started doing some dance. Stamping with their right foot, shuffling forward, the left hand came around almost, and they would crouch down almost like they were cupping imaginary water, which they would throw out into the air, and then the right foot would come up and stamp again.

"DANCE!" all the voices commanded in their strange but perfect harmony. To make the hands pulling and prodding at him leave him alone, he imitated the dance with the others, and immediately the remaining people pulled away to the outer circle.

Belinda, who awkwardly followed the others dancing at his side, said to him, "The dance and the beat sound Native American."

Jesse grunted in agreement and said, "I think we can tell Phil that there is definitely something strange going on in his little corner of nowhere, Michigan."

"Let's just go along with it for now and see what happens," urged Belinda.

Jesse nodded and danced. As with most things, since they had eaten vampire hearts full of the blood of the archangel Jophiel, learning new things came easy to him with angelic grace. They wove, and he stamped and could all but feel the water that their left hand dipped into the stream and flung to the heavens. As the dance became easy, he also realized that the drumbeat was not just a random rhythm but almost a word.

He strained to hear that word. What was the beat saying? He felt himself say the words, "Unk Cekula, Unk Cekula," and glanced at Belinda again to see if she heard it. Their eyes caught each other even as they danced, and he could see her mouth moving, saying the same word over and over, "Unk Cekula."

As he realized she heard it, the fluorescent lights seemed to dim and darken, and shadows seemed to suddenly fill the outer circle of people who beat the drums and stamped their feet to the rhythm. Belinda and the four other couples dipped their hands into invisible water and sent imaginary droplets flying and stamped their feet, all five couples now in perfect harmony.

Jesse tried to see into the swirling shadows that seemed to gather in militia members' outer circle. He knew he could see into darkness at night better than a normal man, but he could see nothing but flowing shadows, like a river of shadows. Then he recognized the shape. The shadows around the outer circle moved like a giant snake.

A new movement drew his eyes to the other dancing couples, and he now saw that smaller shadow snakes seemed to be coiling around the heads of the other dancing couples, moving with the same dancing moves. He remembered the snake on the young man. Had it been real or one of these shadows? Some supernatural evil spirit, he guessed.

In a strained voice, Belinda said, "They are possessed."

"And they are calling the giant mother snake to add us to their team," guessed Jesse before adding. "That kid we grabbed should have said Go Shadow, not Go Blue. He's not a genuine fan of the University of Michigan."

Belinda said nothing in return, and he looked towards her in alarm. A mortal could eat two hearts of power to become enhanced; those with opposing virtues that mirrored each other gave you the most boost. Jesse had eaten two enormously powerful hearts. Belinda had only eaten one, but she also had something else; however, it might not help her fight the giant shadow snake's influence.

"Belinda, get ready to flame on!" Jesse told her, not caring who could hear him. The good news was no one seemed to have their guns at the ready anymore, either confident in their numbers or too caught up in their ritual. He reminded himself the people were just victims. The threat was the giant shadow that seemed to be coiling more and more around the outer circle. He now noticed the head of the creature with what he thought were two glowing eyes.

He turned to Belinda again. She seemed lost in the chant's power. He forcefully said, "I don't think we can wait," pointing at the giant head of the serpent that seemed to be coiling closer and closer to them as it circled. "There is the head of what I am guessing is Unk Cekula," he pointed, forcing himself to stop dancing. "I can't punch or shoot a shadow, but I'm guessing that the flames of Uriel will do wonders."

Belinda, though, seemed not to hear his words and continued the dance. "Frack this crap," said Jesse to himself. His instinct was telling him now or never, and that was likely as not Archangel Jophiel's wisdom shining through. He pulled himself out of the dance, grabbed Belinda's arms, and ran towards the part of the outer circle where he thought he saw a pair of red glowing eyes. Stopping dancing felt like pulling himself out of mud, but he was strong, in full flight or fight mode, always preferring a good fight.

As soon as he pulled Belinda from the dance, he felt her jerk free. "Alright, alright, let's get this mother," she growled, pissed off by her own inability to pull free.

As they staggered toward the shadow of the giant snake, it reared over them and seemed to open a fanged mouth. Jesse thought it would try to swallow them, but then he saw smaller shadow snakes pouring out of his mouth and onto them.

Except that Belinda was suddenly covered in bright burning flames as she called upon Uriel's mantle, and she reached up with her hands at the falling shadows and the small snakes burned. The flames were a gift that Belinda had agreed to host because the Archangel Uriel could not trust herself with them while she was on earth.

Uriel's flames were the three-dimensional expression of the concept of transformation. Against most kinds of supernatural creatures, they seemed like a splendid weapon to Jesse.

Belinda knew that the flames had to touch a creature to affect it. This limited their usefulness, as, in most cases, supernatural creatures were inhumanly strong, and in close quarters, they could tear her apart. That was not a concern here, though, against this shadow. She ran into the darkest part of the giant shadow snake, that seemed to swirl and coil among the men and women of the outer circle, like a human burning torch.

Belinda screamed, "Sade retro Santana! I name you Unk Cekula and send you back to the pit!"

Jesse realized that Belinda was going full-on Exorcist. It shouldn't surprise him; Belinda was brought up profoundly religious and knew more about the Bible and religion than anyone he knew that was not an angel.

Jesse was no good in this kind of fight, but he stayed near as she continued to run into the darkest of the shadow snake, which now seemed to be confused by what was happening. A hiss came from a militia man and woman, and while the drumbeat continued and the four couples continued to dance, it seemed stilted now, no longer in perfect harmony.

"By the Father, the Son, and the Holy Ghost, begone from here and release these poor souls from your foul grip!" the young woman commanded. As she shouted, she reached up, and her hands disappeared into the shadow, but while they never physically touched anything, her flames did, and the angry hissing gained an alarmed note.

Once more, Belinda shouted out her voice ringing true and commanding, "I name you Unk Cekula and by the Flame of Uriel, and in the name of Jesus Christ, I expel you from this world!"

The flames no longer just emanated from Belinda but were running through the shadow coils of the great shadow spirit, consuming it. The sound of hissing from the throats of the militia members now had a tone of panic. If a snake could scream, this is what it would sound like.

In a tone of finality, Belinda's voice rang out, "Begone foul spirit from this place and from these people. Sade retro Santana! In the name of all this is holy, you are banished!" As if in response, the flames that now covered both the great snake's shadows had also spread to the smaller snakes on the militia members' heads. There was a moment of brightness, and then the dim flickering lights strengthened, and the shadow was gone. Belinda immediately withdrew the burning flames of the mantle of Uriel back inside of her.

A moment later, there was quiet and a lot of confusion. "Who are you people?" asked a woman, who, while she used the plural, was giving an ugly look at Belinda. Jesse thought that the good news was that the complete and reasonable question suggested that Belinda had been successful against the evil spirit. The bad news was that Uriel's flame did not fix racism.

"An evil entity possessed you," explained Belinda. "Some Native American evil spirit, I think. Do you all remember anything?" she asked.

When the only one who responded asked, "What are you talking about? Is this some Deep State trick?" Jesse stepped up to Belinda, who seemed to want to have a reasonable conversation, grabbed her arm and started pulling her to the door.

"I want to thank everyone for this tour of the Sparrow Mountain Militia—you folks are great, but it is getting dark, and we have to let our dog out to pee. Have a splendid night!" They hurried down the road toward the main entrance. Belinda did not fight him. They had been through a lot together and trusted each other's instincts.

Luckily, no one seemed to follow them. Clearly, there was some memory loss with the possessing spirits being banished, but that in no way made the people involved less dangerous or saner. These types were always whining about others and were too easy to anger.

"I do feel a little awkward about using a Christian ceremony to banish a Native American spirit, lots of sad history around that," said Belinda.

"Oh, I didn't think of that, but I think this guy was no one's friend. Whether it had gone mad or what. I think your exorcism was definitely appropriate," said Jesse.

"Do you think Mr. Fisher will believe our explanation?" asked Belinda.

"If I were Phil, I wouldn't, but maybe when things calm down, if they calm down. I think these people had too many guns and were doing crazy stuff well before they got themselves possessed."

"Yeah, easy prey for a malignant spirit, but I think we did some good," agreed Belinda.

Jesse nodded, "No angels saved, but yeah, not a terrible night's work."

BACKGROUND FOR
MOTIVATED MILITIA

What historical period did you choose and what attracted you to it?
Modern day, because it is hard to beat such a twisted and dark time

What did you change and what do you see the fallout from it to be?
The Michigan Militia movement was under supernatural influence, which explains its shocking behavior.

What texts were crucial to your research?
Ones on the mythical underground horned serpents of the Muskogee and Souix, such as rockartblog.blogspot.com/2011/04/water-monsters-unktehi-and-uncegila.html

What is a good introduction to this period?
A mix of Jim Butcher's *The Dresden Files* and Neil Gaiman's *American Gods*.

TIPPECANOE AND KENNEDY, TOO

Joseph Cadotte

"Let me tell you about the time I almost killed a president..."
"Again?"
"Shut up. You might finally learn something."

You couldn't tell it from looking at me, but I was young and tall and strong, once. I mean, I'm still fit, and I'm going to stay in independent living until they have to drag me out, but you should have seen me when I was a kid. I had the chin and cheekbones of Charlton Heston and the body of Brando. Back then, before he got fat. People told me, if I was whiter, I could have been a star. The fact that I never could act didn't mean anything. That's how good looking I was.

"I doubt it."
"You weren't there! You don't know!"

Like many of my people, I fought in Vietnam. It wasn't out of a sense of patriotism, or a sense of duty. It was out of a sense of guilt. If I hadn't been such a procrastinator, Kennedy wouldn't have escalated the war. We wouldn't have lost those missile bases in Turkey. All those people in the insane asylums wouldn't be on the street. That megalomaniacal bastard LBJ would never have been president. I don't think you can blame me for Cuba, but an argument could be made that that was my fault, too. Sometimes I feel guilty for what I did, but then I remember that he had a mistress who worked for the Stasi or that he lost us Cuba or the Pentagon Papers, and I just don't care.

I grew up around here, in Cincinnati. Most of my family was on the rez in Oklahoma, but my dad had done well with his GI Bill and bought a house right where we came from, or so he said. I once looked it up, and my ancestors were actually from Greene county, up near Dayton, but given a choice between Dayton and pretty much anywhere else in Ohio, I'd pick Cincinnati, too. Dayton was a hole then and it's a hole now.

People around here call me Paul, and pretty much have most of my life, but my mom named me after my grand, grand, grand-something uncle, Paukeesaa. He was the son of Tecumsah, and that was drilled into me every day from birth until I did what I did. Actually, until I tried to do what I didn't get around to doing until probably too late.

I don't know if you know this, now that we've had a few presidents who haven't died in office, but my grand, grand, grand, grand-something uncle, Tecumsah, was supposed to have laid a curse on the president. Every twenty years, the president who was elected in a year ending in zero would die in office. It started with Harrison, who beat my blah-blah-blah uncle back at Tippecanoe. He even won the office because of it, which I think was racist, but times were different. Harrison also died because he caught pneumonia, but we claimed it as our own because maybe the curse did have something to do with it.

After that, like clockwork, every twenty years, the President would die before finishing his term. Booth, Guiteau, Czolgolsz, those drooling idiots kept it going, but Harding died of a heart attack and Roosevelt almost broke the curse altogether. We couldn't let whoever won in '60 make it out alive. It would be a stain on the family honor.

I was so glad when Nixon lost. Sure, he would have been a better president, especially with all of his civil rights work, even if that racist bastard LBJ killed that bill in the Senate, but he never would have won in '68 if we had had to kill him and then we would have had no EPA, no open China, no university integration, and we'd still be on the gold standard.

JFK, though, he was a crook and a rapist and everyone knew it. It was obvious from back when he was senator and he had his speechwriter write *Profiles in Courage* for him. My sister thought he was cute and wanted to go see him when he came to Cincinnati on a campaign stop, but dad put his foot down. Later, much later (because we didn't talk about such things back then), we found out he had gotten some girls from her high school into bed. One of them went away for a couple months.

People in my generation seem to all have forgotten what an awful, drugged-up, incompetant scumbag he was. Oliver Stone made him into a cottage industry. The guy was almost up for impeachment before he died and might have had Marilyn Monroe killed, but the bastard got assassinated, and all of that was forgotten and forgiven.

I mean, I was there, but I always thought the best theory about his assassination came from an old BBC show, *Red Dwarf,* where he went back in time to kill himself because he knew what was coming. That or Joe Dimaggio and Arthur Miller teamed up to do it.

There was talk in the family of making Tecumsah's curse stick to Kennedy. It was always in the abstract, like I said, of making absolutely sure that it would come true, but assassinating someone like Kennedy would actually be a mitzvah, as my nurse Sam says. He's a Christian like me, but he uses a lot of Yiddishisms. I think it's because he watches Seinfeld reruns almost exclusively. During the 1960 campaign and every moment after, my mom and dad were going after him. Any time he'd appear on television, they'd flip their lids and we'd get an earful.

The whole thing was up to me. My dad had been in the military, so his prints were on record. Our cousins in Oklahoma were always in trouble with the law, mostly for just breathing near white people, so they weren't any better. No one even thought of my sister or my mother—it simply wasn't done at the time. Even so, after Marilyn died, my sister would have pulled the trigger without a thought. Marilyn had been her idol, until she got into Debbie Harry and then Taylor Swift, which she really liked from her Zumba thing. The very minute she heard about Marilyn, she grabbed the gun I'd been working on and was halfway to the Greyhound stop when we caught up to her. We really should have let her do the job. The Cuban Missile Crisis would never have happened without that idiot in office making things worse and we wouldn't have sent "advisors" to Vietnam.

Some people, mostly the sort of people who say they were hippies but really weren't, have told me that I was brainwashed, but then I talk to older people who remember what JFK was really like or the young people who only know him from history, and I think, sure they might have a point. I think I would have come around to the same way of thinking regardless. His death wasn't a loss of innocence unless you were a very specific age, and even then, you had to ignore a lot of shady stuff.

I wasn't in any record except Selective Service and my high school's graduation records when he took office. My mother, she gave me an old Brown Bess that had been salvaged from Tippecanoe. She felt that it would be appropriate that a gun that had been used against us would kill a president. I want to tell her that it was a mistake, but I understand her thinking, and, once I grew up a bit, after I joined the Army, I stopped using that musket as an excuse for my pussyfooting around.

Like most kids back then, I knew how to shoot, but that old beast was different. It was almost five feet long and weighed ten pounds. I have to admit, a lot of my early procrastination came from being scared of the thing. The fact that it hadn't been maintained since before the Civil War didn't help.

The money was also a reason I was dragging my heels. My parents told me that they would help me make ends meet while I practiced. My cousins also pitched in. Every so often, I would get "drunk" in front of some Cubans or Republicans or some Civil Rights folk that had just had Hoover go after them, and they would often pitch in to buy bullets or a bus ticket to DC or whatever I was selling. I want to make it clear that I never actually got drunk. Every so often, I would have a sip of whiskey or scotch or vodka, but only at weddings and funerals. I'm not a dime-store Indian stereotype. Sure, I smoked, but who didn't? The air was thick in those bars. I couldn't do anything fancy, like blow smoke rings, but I would gesture and leave trails in the smoke with my stories, like I was sculpting the air into abstracts of my message. Thank Christ that I didn't end up with cancer.

It did take a lot of money to get the Brown Bess operational. I could have bought a replica that worked fine and took modern ammunition for much less, but, at first, my mom insisted. It didn't take long for me to realize that fixing that thing was a rabbit hole

I could throw a lot of time into. Especially as I could realistically show that every fix made me have to relearn how to properly shoot the thing.

Telling stories and getting the Brown Bess up to snuff was how I spent '61.

I fell in love in '62. I had dated before, and fancied myself quite the ladies' man, but I had never truly been in love. It was with a small blonde girl named Linda who was going through a rebellious phase, and the more her mom disapproved, the more she clung to me. Her father didn't care about the race thing, but he was a die-hard union man, the kind who voted twice in every election and did everything he could to keep the Negros (although he didn't say Negro) from good jobs, and my family being notoriously anti-Kennedy didn't help matters.

Needless to say, our parents didn't get along at all. The fact that we went to the same church didn't help—they saw too much of each other every week. I was a year out of high school and she was ending the year as a junior, and the fact that I was living off of my parents made me look like a mooch. I don't blame them feeling that way about me now, but I did, then.

Like most young love stories, it was full of passion and took up far too much of our time. Everything seemed far too important and life-shaking. We were young and restless and took it way too far. We broke it off several times in the way that young lovers do, and I didn't cry, but I should have, each time. We got back together each time, though. Eventually, after a summer spent separated, with her staying with her cousins on a farm in Illinois and me trying and failing to prepare to kill the president, we got back together and both of our parents blessed us on the condition that I got a job and she would graduate with honors. I started at a gas station during the day, when she was at school, and, for the first time, was able to support myself. I still lived with my parents, but no one had a problem with it. I was supposed to be saving for a home for Linda, after all.

Everything looked good for us, but the more I worked and the more she studied, the more we drifted apart. By the time she graduated, in May of '63, we hadn't really spent more than an hour together except on weekends, and then we were too exhausted to even talk much. When she told me she got into OSU for the fall, it seemed like a relief, as much as I wanted to be sad. I spent a month moping about.

A bit ago, I found Linda on Myspace. We chatted quite a bit and sent emails full of photos and our families. She had married and divorced and married again. After school, she went on to be first a clerk, then, after her divorce, started her own business, where she met her husband. We talked about setting up one of my grandchildren with one of hers, but nothing came of it. Finally, one day, after we had both switched over to Facebook, she just stopped answering texts. A couple of days later, her page changed to a memorial site, and that's when I actually cried over Linda.

"Grandma never liked you telling the Linda part of the story."
"She said it was fine!"
"She said it was fine the way a woman means 'fine', not the way a man means it."

That month of moping brought me into the summer of '63. I had bought a Sony TR-63 to listen to as a consolation present to myself, and was listening to it nonstop. I especially liked all the beach music, since I hadn't seen one outside of a trip to Lake Erie. I was a huge Beach Boys fan. When *Pet Sounds* was released a few years later, I was all over it. You know, people actually use thingies on their computers to make music sound like an old radio?

"Vinyl is very fashionable, grandpa."

"What, LPs? We would've given an arm and a leg to get rid of those pops, squawks, and all that fuzz. Y'all are strange."

Anyway, the entire time I was with Linda, my parents had been on my case about Kennedy. After Marilyn died, so was my sister. I had been so wrapped up in her that I hadn't even heard them. As my funk ended, I nutted up and started practicing in earnest with Brown Bess. I still wasn't terribly accurate at any decent range, but that was more down to the fact that it was a smoothbore musket and hitting anything was more a matter of chance than I'd like. I guess I'd have to wait until I saw the whites of Kennedy's eyes.

On November 22nd, I was in Dallas. We had been following JFK's movements as best we could through the news, and, once the trip was announced in September, we decided that was when and where I'd get him. In late October, I drove down to Dallas, and I parked myself in a cheap boarding house. Suffice it to say, it wasn't ideal. I had to be in by curfew and the radio was always turned to country stations. I don't mind country as much now, but they refused to play my "long hair" music. The food wasn't great, either. It was bland and the portions were too small. I quickly learned that outside food was as welcome as loose women, which was defined as any woman who would talk to me.

It didn't take long for me to make contact with the local Shoshone community, which was sparse, hoping for them to put me up. While they expressed some sympathy, apparently they had heard about my schmoozing back in '61 and were wary of helping me. I burned through a lot of time in that room. I had spent some years waiting, quite happily, but now that I actually was motivated, all the waiting ate at me.

That room was my base of operations, and I watched every bit of news I could and read every paper from cover to cover. I had clippings everywhere and my fingers were always stained with ink. During the day, when the soaps and game shows were on, I would walk the Dallas parade routes, the ones that other politicians used. People, mostly the same sort who think the "magic bullet" is a thing, think that Dealey Plaza was out of the way for the motorcade, but it was often part of the routes that parades took. It was the "heart of Dallas", at least that's what the local librarian said. Also, that was on a sign somewhere.

The County Records and Central Court buildings would have been perfect, but there was no way the Brown Bess wouldn't be noticed, nor could I just wait there until the parade came by, especially without being hassled and picked up for loitering. However, the book depository was right there. Trying to figure out what it was for, and how to get into it, was how I met the librarian. Her name was Margaret or Marjorie or something, but she went by Peggie. I don't mean to make it seem like I seduced her or that she was part of the whole thing. She was just nice and very useful and didn't turn away when she saw me, like a few of her colleagues did. She's probably been dead for years.

I figured that I wouldn't be able to shoot from there, although it was the perfect sniper's nest. It was under construction, and there were a lot of men about. I figured one lone Indian would stand out in the crowd, but it was definitely my first choice. On the 22nd, when I got there, I just tried the door, couldn't get in, and crossed the street to sit on the grass, under the trees, near the pergola. Later, some guy would call it a knoll, but it was really more of just a hummock between streets.

"Those are the same thing."

"What?"

"A hummock and a knoll. They are synonyms."

"I never heard of a knoll before the whole 'grassy knoll' thing. It was a hummock."

I had a picnic lunch and spread out a blanket. I was going to cover the Brown Bess, but there were a lot of people coming and going, and not a few of them admired it. It really was in pretty good condition. More than a couple wanted to fire it, and I let them. I think that was the smartest thing I did that day. If I had had to ditch it, there would have been far too many fingerprints on it to trace it to me. On the other hand, I ran out of ammunition faster than I expected. It's not like black powder, the right sort of paper wadding, and properly sized lead balls were things I could just run down the street and pick them up at the local five-and-dime. I was down to two shots before I noticed.

Around half past twelve, the first car of the motorcade appeared. It was filled with cops, and it was gone before Kennedy's car turned the corner. I moved into position, which took a bit of time in that crowd.

I loaded the gun. I aimed. No one bothered me. Maybe they thought it was a protest. There were a lot of people in that crowd who were angry at that crooked bastard, and for a lot of good reasons. The Brown Bess didn't have a second sight, but I used the lug that was supposed to hold the bayonet on as one. I waited until he rode right into view and he crossed my line of sight. I fired.

There was no crack from the bullet because the ball went far too slow. It was just a flash and a puff of smoke. The musket didn't sound like real gun, and the people around me clapped me on the back and cheered, thinking that I had just set off a firework, because that was what it sounded like. I admit that I was too excited and I knew that I had missed the moment I pulled the trigger.

I dropped the gun and started to reload. I heard one shot, and everyone looked toward the car. I had the ramrod in my hand as I heard the second shot. I threw it away, jerked the Brown Bess to my shoulder, aimed, and fired, just as I heard the third and last shot.

That commie, Oswald, had poached my kill.

As I was packing everything up as quickly as I could, I saw the wad on the ground, with the bullet a few paces behind it, and a lot of unburnt powder. I had rushed too much and the thing hadn't been properly packed. I had literally shot my wad.

In the end, it didn't really matter. I wasn't hailed as a conquering hero when I got home, and Linda's dad, who remembered all the times I had bragged that I was going to kill Kennedy, took a swipe at me, and I let him, but Tecumsah's curse stood, and it would until Reagan survived Hinckley's assassination attempt. Even so, Reagan was never the same afterward, so maybe the curse was just spent and forgotten, much the way my great-great-great-blah-blah-blah-uncle was. Much the way I am.

"Grandpa you tell that story every time we see you. How many times do I have to say I'm sorry we missed your birthday last year?"

"I don't know. Did you get me the new Taylor Swift?"

"Auntie asked me the same thing. It's not out until next year."

"I don't think she could ever top 1989, but I can keep hoping. Do your kids want to play with Brown Bess?"

"No. They can't. Not since you gave it to them loaded. You know that."

"If the wrong guy gets elected, you know that one of them is going to have to get the curse going again. They better practice."

"That didn't work on me last time, and it won't work now."

"We'll see."

BACKGROUND FOR
TIPPECANOE AND KENNEDY, TOO

What historical period did you choose and what attracted you to it?

I chose the 1960s, as it was the last time an American president was successfully assassinated.

What did you change and what do you see the fallout from it to be?

I added a mild possibly mystical element that has haunted American presidential deaths since 1840. Part of my goal was to make it as plausible as possible, so nothing in American history will have changed.

What texts were crucial to your research?

Jan Brunvald wrote about many American urban legends in his multiple works on the subject. Tecumseh's Curse was one of them. The excellent site Snopes, his spiritual successor, has an in-depth article on the subject: snopes.com/fact-check/the-curse-of-tecumseh/

Many books on unsolved mysteries and other books examining fringe theories also go in depth on the JFK assassination, although their credibility varies between "accurate reporting of various conspiracies" to "aliens did it".

The myth of a second shooter has been debunked many times over. The *Mythbusters* TV show has covered it, for example, and so has *Red Dwarf,* which has the most plausible alternative theories that I've seen.

What is a good introduction to this period?
Despite the fact that it is almost entirely a work of fiction, Oliver Stone's "JFK" is a fun alternate history. Although I saw it entirely after the story was finished, the second season of the *Umbrella Academy* does a very good job discussing race relations and other pressing issues of the day, although it ignores JFK's massive lack of concern (at best) regarding them. Many science fiction works of the day cover the gestalt of the early sixties quite well, from the execrable *Stranger in a Strange Land* to the far superior (and actually readable) works like *The Forever War, Dune,* and *Squares of the City.*

AUTHOR BIOS

MICHAEL DAVID ANDERSON

Michael David Anderson is the author of the Teddy Dormer novels, *Teddy* and *Wake*, their companion piece *Desynchrony*, and the haunted house novel *In the House of Wolves*. He possesses degrees in both Psychology and English. He was born in East Tennessee in 1985 and currently resides in Florida with his fiancée Christine. In addition to writing horror and suspense novels, Anderson is a poet, gamer, and the creator of the *Authors in Abstract* podcast. His dogs, Bandit and Rory, serve as a constant distraction from his writing.

VONNIE WINSLOW CRIST

Vonnie Winslow Crist, SFWA, HWA, is author of *The Enchanted Dagger, Owl Light, The Greener Forest, Murder on Marawa Prime*, and other books. Her fiction appears in *Amazing Stories, Cast of Wonders, Lost Signals of the Terran Republic, Cirsova Magazine, Chilling Ghost Short Stories, Killing It Softly 2, Insignia 2020: Best Asian Speculative Fiction*, and elsewhere. Born in the Year of the Dragon, Vonnie believes the world is still filled with magic, mysteries, and miracles. For more info, visit vonniewinslowcrist.com/

JAMES DORR

James Dorr's most recent book is a novel-in-stories from Elder Signs Press, *Tombs: A Chronicle Of Latter-Day Times Of Earth*. His book, *The Tears of Isis*, was a 2013 Bram Stoker Award® finalist for Fiction Collection. Other books include *Strange Mistresses: Tales Of Wonder And Romance, Darker Loves: Tales Of Mystery And*

Regret, and his all-poetry *Vamps (A Retrospective)*. Dorr is also an active member of HWA and SFWA.

SCOTT HARPER

The son of an English teacher and a cop, Scott Harper grew up reading stories of monsters and super heroes. His writing style was influenced by the works of Bram Stoker, Marv Wolfman, and John Steakley; and his stories have appeared in a wide variety of speculative fiction venues as well as indie comics. When not at the gym, Scott spends his time reading and writing in his collector's man cave, surrounded by books, models and action figures. He lives in California with his wife, son and two dogs.

GIL HOUGH

Gil Hough was born in Detroit, Michigan and raised on the waters of lake St. Clair. After settling in Knoxville, Tennessee, he spent four years organizing Appalachian communities, then worked as the Tennessee Director of Renewable Programs at the Southern Alliance for Clean Energy, until he moved on to developing renewable projects with RSI Entech LLC. He is a founding member of TenneSEIA (Tennessee Solar Energy Industries Association). For more of Jesse, Belinda, and Scooby, read or listen to the novellas of *The Throne of Hearts* by Gil Hough, gilhough.com.

ELIZABETH KIDDER

Elizabeth Kidder is an author, illustrator, and teacher living in Tennessee with her husband, two cats, and a collection of books constantly outgrowing its shelf space. Previous works include her first novel, *ColorBlind*, and the short story "NightMares" from the alternate history anthology *Beyond Steampunk*. You can view her work on Instagram @ekidderillustrator and elizabethkidder.com.

TIM LIEDER

Tim Lieder has been published in several markets including *Shock Totem, Saturday Evening Post,* and *Tales from the Crust.* He lives in New York. Additionally he owns and operates Dybbuk Press through which he has published nine titles including *King David & the Spiders from Mars.* His patreon is at patreon.com/timlieder.

BILL MAXWELL

A third-generation Southern Californian, Bill Maxwell works in the video game, tabletop RPG, and LARP industries. In addition to almost three decades as a writer, he has been a script doctor, game designer, a director, second-unit producer, and an editor. The horror novel *Shadowpath* was his first full-length book. *The Sunset Call* is a collection of terrifying stories about faeries. His second novel, *Silence in the Chapel,* is in the hands of the publisher. wtmaxwell.com.

JASON J. McCUISTON

A Writers of the Future semi-finalist, Jason has published stories in over a dozen anthologies, magazines, websites, and podcasts, including Pole to Pole Publishing's *Not Far From Roswell, StoryHack Magazine, Crimson Streets,* and *Tales to Terrify.* His debut novel, *Project Notebook,* will appear in summer of 2020, published by Tell-Tale Press. A native Tennessean, he now lives in South Carolina with his wife and two dogs.

JAMES PALMER

James Palmer is an award-nominated writer of science fiction and pulp adventure. He is perhaps best known as the co-creator and editor of the shared world, alternate history giant monster anthologies *Monster Earth* and its sequels. James is also the author of four novellas in the Shadow Council Archives series from Falstaff Books: *The Depths of Time, Shadows Over London, The Dream Key,* and *The Map of Time.* For a free ebook, visit JamesPalmerBooks.net.

WHITNEY "AIRPANTS" PETELKA

A cemetery caretaker who bills herself as the "poor man's Renaissance woman", Petelka writes, creates art, podcasts, and tries to live her best Southern gothic life. She and her husband dwell in Knoxville, Tennessee with two cats, a dog, a rat, a snake, and two horses. When not tending to the dead, Petelka enjoys pop-up camping and afternoon naps. You can reach Whitney at airpants.get@gmail.com, or patreon.com/airpants.

THOMAS VAUGHN

Thomas Vaughn is a speculative fiction writer whose work encompasses literary horror and dark magical realism. He is a byproduct of the debris field of rural Arkansas, a place he calls the archive of pain. His recent novella, *The Ethereal Transit Society,* can be found on Bad Dream Entertainment. When he is not writing fiction, he poses as a college professor whose research focuses on apocalyptic rhetoric and doomsday cults. Feel free to visit him at brokentransmitter.com.

SALLY SMITH

Sally Smith graduated in 1996 from Maryville College with a BA in Fine Arts & English Lit. Since then, she has published a book of poetry and worked painting everything from people to buildings to cars (and pretty much anything else you can imagine). Her current city (and place of origin) is Knoxville, Tennessee.

EDITOR BIOS

JOSEPH CADOTTE

Joseph is a game designer and lead editor at his family's educational software company, Innovative Learning Solutions. He also founded Old Sins as a literary cooperative and an alternative to many mainstream presses. Joseph has authored two novels and one graphic novel, all hard science fiction, with more on the way. He lives in the lovely resort town of Wilmington, NC with his dog, Dwight "Doggie" Eisenhower, his cat, Scout, his wife, Cordelia, and their son, Jacob.

CORDELIA NORRIS

Designer and illustrator Cordelia Norris runs the award-winning design + marketing studio, Luna Creative. She specializes in working with mission-driven organizations that make a positive environmental or social impact. Owing to her background in book design and love of type, she frequently finds herself designing and editing books authored by various family members, usually against her better judgement. You can view her studio's work at lunacreates.com and her paintings at etsy.com/shop/LocalLoveBoutique.

www.ingramcontent.com/pod-product-compliance
Lightning Source LLC
Chambersburg PA
CBHW021142190726
48288CB00008B/2782